SECRETS FROM THE TEACHERS' LOUNGE

To Cheryl

wheresoever you go,
go with all of
your heart!

Mona Green

Mona Green

ISBN: 0692663983
ISBN 13: 9780692663981

CONTENTS

DEDICATION

I dedicate this book to Kris, Joey, Gay, Lora, Pat, Peter, and Winnie.
Thank you for your help and encouragement when I needed it most.
Thank you, Bill, for listening.

"We each need to make peace with our memories. We have all done things that make us flinch."

—Surya Das

Hey, I should write a book. I said these words often in the teachers' lounge.

Someone would say, "No one will believe you!" And then we'd all laugh.

Toward the end of my public school teaching career, I knew that there were stories in me that needed a bigger audience—I had shared some stories with my fellow teachers and belly laughs, as well as tears, with my husband and children. But I wanted to show the world what really goes on in schools. I also believed that writing about my experience, as a memoir, would be cathartic.

Even though I had stories to write, that didn't mean I was a writer. I had to convince myself of what I often told my students—a writer is a person who writes. I considered my writing skills to be inferior and it was really difficult in the beginning. I did enroll in a few helpful online memoir classes and read some terrific memoirs. I found a writing group for retired people at the local university. My instructor told me that she saw some promise in my writing. That was all I needed—a reason to believe in myself. That writing group helped me stay focused and disciplined.

Secrets from the Teachers' Lounge is a fictional memoir. Which is to say that ninety-five percent of what is in these pages is true. I will leave it to my readers to determine what isn't. I should note that I changed the names to protect the innocent, or the guilty, because my intent is not to hurt or shame anyone, especially children. Having said that, you can be sure that the "me" in my memoir is authentic.

When I first began to write, I imagined my memoir to be a hilarious piece of work. But as I continued, it became clear to me that the stories that had the biggest impact on my life were the ones that had dealt with the parts of life that hurt the most—parents died, kids mourned, teachers were berated. Not everyone behaved appropriately. Nor did I. Be prepared to read some heart-wrenching narratives.

Secrets from the Teachers' Lounge is not about a heroine disguised as a teacher. Or a school administrator disguised as a savior, as many teacher memoirs are. I have come to realize that I was often unreasonable, critical and way too sensitive. There were times when I was too compassionate. I was often amused when I should have been chagrined. At times, I wanted to crawl and hide under the nearest desk—and I probably should have. And I did things that I'm not proud of.

There is no doubt that my education in parochial schools colored my adult world and I share some flashbacks in this memoir. Often, what happened to the kids in my classroom and school brought me right back to that little French Canadian girl in the

Air Force blue uniform that I was. In a sense, my memoir is a time-travel experiment.

As a special education teacher, I taught in two urban school systems. As an administrator, I worked in two suburban systems—one wealthy, the other predominately working class. My experience in public schools taught me that the students and their parents, no matter their socio-economic status, were driven by the same desires. Whether they spoke little English. Whether they lived in a motel. It just didn't matter. They all wanted respect, the opportunity to thrive, and to be safe and happy. I also discovered that you will find the real heroes where you least expect them.

FIRST DAY OF SCHOOL

The first day of my special education teaching career is a day that I will never forget.

The school was in a neighborhood of sad, sagging tenements, long vacated by working class French-Canadians and now populated by families from Puerto Rico and the Dominican Republic. It was an imposing brick monstrosity built as a parochial school in 1922 and used as an overflow school for the streams of kids, typically six hundred per year, who were flooding the school system. The city could barely keep up with the demand.

The principal, Joan Rappaport, and her twelve teachers faced 250 brown faces and five white ones lingering in the staff's parking lot. Most of the kids were chasing each other around and in-between the cars, shouting in Spanish. Joan had a whistle, and she blew it forcefully to get the kids' attention, but she might as well have been blowing on the hair of her arm for all the attention she generated.

Joan tried blowing the whistle several more times, and with each unsuccessful attempt she pursed her thin lips and shook her head from side to side disgustedly. Finally, she turned her gaze to Bobbie Robles, the helmet-headed curriculum coordinator, who was peering out of the cracked window of her office at the school-yard bedlam. Joan caught Bobbie's attention, lifted her arm slightly, and pretended to be ringing a bell. In no time, Bobbie rushed outside with a large old-fashioned ding-dong bell.

A pimply-faced seventh-grade girl with frizzy hair ran up to Bobbie and tried to steal the bell out of her hand. Bobbie pushed her hand away as though she were shoving back an attack dog. The girl, despite being totally inappropriate, looked shocked that Bobbie reacted so forcefully.

"Yo, don't touch me!" she said.

Her friends applauded. "You go Maria! You go Maria!" They were clearly delighted that the girl had managed to humiliate the hapless Bobbie, now even more determined to show them who was boss.

I spotted several teachers smirking, their hands covering their mouths, as Bobbie morphed from bewildered to beady-eyed angry. With all the noise and commotion, she knew that rounding up one or several of these girls for a trip to the office would be daunting and unproductive. She zigzagged through the lot attempting to corral the kids into the small, open area where Joan stood, hugging her clipboard to her chest.

By this time, the teachers had sidled up to a blue Honda Civic. They held oak tag cards with scribbled grade numbers on them. Bobbie shook the bell in sharp, quick spurts, and this time, everybody stopped in their tracks and gave Joan their un-divided attention.

"Grade three! Come to me. Now." Thirty third graders elbowed their way to where she stood. "Ms. Junes, take your class to their room!"

Ms. Junes, hopping to it, did her best to hold up her sign while requesting that the kids form an orderly line, but they barreled ahead of her and charged into the building like shoppers on Black Friday looking for a midnight deal at Wal-Mart.

Finally, all that was left in the makeshift schoolyard were Jimmy Day, who was the school's other special education teacher, our seven students, and me. Several overweight girls with push-up bras stood clustered near the far end of the parked cars, mocking Joan's bell ringing.

"Yo, stop it Maria," shouted one of the girls. When I glanced over, I saw that Maria, the bell snatcher, was one of my students. The other one, Yonatan, a fourth grader, was twirling about, jittery and out of control.

"Yonaton Hernandez and Maria Garcia," Joan shouted. Yonaton seemed relieved that he had finally been claimed by someone and came over to stand beside me. He hopped up and down, his en-thusiasm totally overwhelming him. "Are you my new teacher? Are you my new teacher?" he asked.

"Yes, yes I am. I'm Mrs. Green." And then with the most enthu-siasm I could muster for this human wind-up toy, I murmured: "It's going to be a great year."

I glanced at Maria, who was doing her best to ignore me. Who could blame her? Ridiculing adults was a lot more fun than going up to a classroom with me, Yonaton, and the venerable Iris Moran, the elderly teacher's aide who was surely waiting for us.

"Come on Maria, time to head up," I said, but Maria didn't budge. After what *she* considered a decent amount of time, perhaps thirty seconds, she finally sauntered over to join Yonaton and me for our march to our third-floor classroom. In no time, Yonaton raced ahead, taking the worn, wooden stairs two at time.

We finally reached the third floor where three fifth graders were loitering in the doorway of our classroom. One, a tall, lean boy, was trying to get a hair pick out of the shorter one's hair, while the one with the hair pick was flailing away in an attempt to keep his pick right where he wanted. The third kid smirked when I approached.

"Don't you boys belong in your classroom right about now?" I asked.

"No, the teacher isn't doing anything," said the shorter kid.

"Why are you here and not where you belong?" I asked.

"We came to see my cousin," said one of them.

"Well, I don't see anyone's cousin here," I informed him. "So I guess it's best that you all move on to where you belong."

All of a sudden, sensing that victory could be his, the tall kid reached past me, grabbed the pick and all three students dashed down the corridor. As I struggled to regain my footing, I spotted Joan rounding the corner, the clipboard still glued to her chest. The tall boy slammed into her left side, sending Joan crashing backwards onto the floor.

"Oh my God!" I yelled and ran to her. She hastily rearranged her splayed legs into a modicum of propriety, and by the time I reached her she was patting the floor in search of her glasses and muttering about kids running in the halls when they should be in their classrooms.

"I tried to get them to go to their classrooms because they were horsing around but they didn't listen," I told her.

Joan looked at me askance.

"*Obviously*," she sneered. Joan held on to my arm so she could get on her feet and she pulled her skirt down with an impatient tug.

"You need to move on," she chided. "Your kids shouldn't be alone."

"I'm sorry about this, Joan. I guess I didn't handle any of this the way I should have."

It was at this moment that I realized that I wasn't in a real school. The day was forty minutes old and I had already seen a student snatch a bell out of a teacher's hand and watched the school principal pushed to the floor. The principal was blaming me for being knocked down, students thought that they could go in and out of classrooms at will, and the dress code was non-existent. This couldn't be a typical public school, I thought. No way. How would anything ever get done?

Why I was confused was no mystery. My first twelve years of schooling were spent in Catholic schools, where we rarely stepped out of line, never mind expressed an opinion. With fifty and sixty kids in one classroom, a nun didn't have time to deal with kids who refused to behave. Students and teachers seemed to understand that we had serious business to tend to which was learning to read and write. And I, like all the other kids, thought being in the presence of the nuns and getting any attention at all, was a privilege indeed.

There were many times when I served as a nun's Sherpa, carrying books, supplies, chairs and boxes up and down long staircases. One day, Sister Catherine directed me to go to her classroom to get her "rubbers," those black rubber half-boots that people wore over their shoes in the fifties. I rushed to get them from under her desk as fast as I could, so that I wouldn't miss much more of my recess. When I returned, I knelt in front of her as she lifted her right foot, and then her left, so that I could put the rubbers on her size eleven foot, while she engaged in a conversation with the diminutive Sister Edward. Sister Catherine thought nothing of lifting her feet for personal service, as though she were being tended to by a lowly man servant, and until now, when I flashback to that time some fifty years ago, neither had I. I remember it as if it happened just last week.

Every day after school, I begged for the privilege of clapping erasers. The minuscule particles of chalk dust snaked their way into my nostrils, throat and lungs, and caused me to erupt into fits of sneezing and coughing and choking. As uncomfortable as I was, it never occurred to me to refuse to stop clapping the erasers. I knew my "place" and I almost even liked my "place" because the nuns made the job of clapping the erasers seem so special.

"Who wants to please Jesus and clean the erasers after school?" the nun would ask. I would raise my hands and wave them wildly, praying to be selected so Jesus would love me even more than I knew He already did.

"Now aren't you a good girl doing Jesus's work?" she would say to my back as my hands slammed against each other, hanging outside the tall windows.

I didn't resent my life as a child-indentured servant, and my most cherished fantasy as a child was that someday a child would revere me and recognize that being my personal handmaiden was indeed a privilege.

It didn't look like my childish fantasies were going to be even a remote reality in this school, that was for sure.

I didn't want someone putting boots on my feet, or elbowing other kids out of the way to get me a pen from my desk. I just wanted to feel like I was a real teacher in a real school.

I felt very much like Alice, a blind patient who resided in a nursing home where I worked after graduating from college. She'd flail her arms over her head whenever she was awake, in anticipation of being attacked by what she could not see.

A WARRIOR COMES HOME

"Tell Mrs. Green what happened. Now's your chance to get to the bottom of this."

Mr. Theriault's voice was pitched and angry. He sat slouched in his chair with his arms folded, legs spread wide.

"I can't remember exactly," said Mason. He looked down at his hands and didn't make eye contact with either one of us.

"What do you mean, you don't remember? You remembered in the car! Don't be a wimp because you're here with Mrs. G!"

Mr. Theriault's intimidating words were matched by army fatigues that were bunched up over scuffed war-weary boots. I sneaked a peek at his left hand to see if a wedding ring was still on his finger. I had heard that Mrs. Theriault had left him and taken the kids to live with her mother recently even though he had just returned from Iraq. His homecoming was the talk of the town for days. Everyone at the school gushed when his five-year-old daughter dropped her magic markers to rush into his outstretched arms, but few noticed that his wife stood in the back of the room, her face expressionless.

He and Mason, a sixth grader, had been seated in my office for ten minutes. Both of us had been trying to get Mason to provide details about a bullying incident. I anticipated the morning buzzer going off any minute; I didn't want Mason missing his math class, especially because he was failing.

Mason was a tiny guy. I mistook him for an elementary student when he arrived at the middle school; I even checked his records to be sure he belonged. He had a thick shock of black hair shaped in a bowl cut. His slight overbite made him look impish when he smiled. I loved when he smiled. He didn't smile often.

"Do I have to tell Mrs. G because you're a coward? What's wrong with you anyway? You're not the son I raised." Mr. Theriault was on a roll.

Mason was silent. He snuck a side-glance at me.

"Mason, would you feel better talking alone with Mr. M? You seem a little unsure of yourself right now," I said. Mr. M, the school psychologist, ate lunch with Mason every day. Despite having been in school for almost five months, Mason still felt uncomfortable in the cafeteria. He refused to even enter the cafeteria because he insisted all the kids were looking at him and making fun of him, especially the ones who knew him from fifth grade. Although I had spent hours investigating Mason's allegations, I had yet to find any evidence of this.

"There will be no talking to Mr. M," said Mr. Theriault. "He doesn't need no shrink. What's with schools these days? Everyone needs a shrink? I never had no shrink! I'm trying to help the kid but he's not cooperating. He doesn't know how to cooperate."

I'd heard this diatribe before from him and had come to expect it. I would have had no problem investigating the accusations of bullying, except that Mason had fabricated his fair share of stories. Before I spent hours trying to find the truth and a culprit, I wanted basic facts.

"Don't think that I'm going to tell Mrs. G for you," said Mr. Theriault. "Listen up, Mason. It's time for you to man up! At least tell her what happened if you don't want to say who it is!"

"I don't remember."

He was stuck. He didn't want to lie to me. But he had lied to the warrior who sought justice.

"OK!" Mr. Theriault yelled. "You want to be like that? Be like that. But don't come crying to me the next time someone bullies you. I fought hard for this damn country but I'm *done* fighting for you!"

Mr. Theriault pulled himself to a standing position and pressed his hands into the table. He leaned forward so that he was mere inches from my face. I could smell coffee on his breath. He was that close.

His eyes held my gaze as he said, "And if you want advice from me, stop babying this kid. You people tiptoe around him like he's going to fall apart if he has to face a little reality."

No wonder Mason was afraid of him. I was afraid of him.

ANOTHER WARRIOR
COMES HOME

The sixth graders complained about Daniel Arpin from the very first day of school. The litany of his transgressions involved pushing, gossiping, flinging rubber bands in the cafeteria and making fun of kids who were overweight or socially inept.

Although we were concerned about Daniel's behaviors, the teachers and I were worried more about the frequency of his offenses: Daniel was in my office on a daily basis. It was almost as if he enjoyed getting in trouble.

Whenever I called him into my office, he'd breeze in like I had invited him to a neighborhood cocktail party. His face would light up and he'd say, "Hello Mrs. G, I'm in trouble again. I'm telling you, it's not my fault, but I'll accept my punishment. I know I have to."

When kids were sent to my office, I typically would sit at my conference table to help them to feel at ease. But with Daniel,

I wanted to make sure he knew who was boss, so I stayed parked behind my desk. He'd pull his chair as close as he could, then look at pictures of my children or play with my stapler. After I admonished him, he would typically tell me he was hungry and ask if I had something to eat. I kept the bottom drawer of my desk chock full of granola bars and Goldfish, and soon I was filling my stash based on Daniel's preferred treats.

I knew that he was playing me for a sucker, but I also knew that this behavior was not normal. Daniel would pay a compliment to my hair, my clothes and my office décor. I had to admit that I found him engaging. Sixth-grade boys don't typically care to spend time with a sixty-year-old assistant principal unless there was something very wrong, and something was clearly wrong with Daniel.

I made a few phone calls to the elementary school and spoke with the adjustment counselor there. He told me that the whereabouts of Daniel's biological father were unknown and that his mother had moved to Maine after her divorce from Daniel's stepfather, Greg. She apparently neglected to take her children with her. He didn't know when the father had deserted Daniel. He also suspected Daniel's father didn't even know he existed. The father who had been caring for Daniel was Greg. To make matters more confusing, Daniel often referred to Sherry, Greg's new girlfriend, as Mom, although Sherry made it clear that she was *not* his mother. Sherry and Greg both served two tours of duty in Iraq, and while they were gone, Greg's parents cared for Daniel and his nine-year-old brother.

I didn't meet Greg until a few months into the school year. The principal had called the Department of Children and Families after Daniel complained of being hit with a belt. Greg insisted on a meeting with the principal and me "to clear his good name" and to tell us about Daniel. At that point the DCF had screened out the case and found no evidence of abuse.

Greg arrived promptly at the appointed time and said that he was unemployed. He explained it was due to medical issues related to his military service but did not elaborate. Like Mr. Theriault, he was dressed in his army fatigues and sported a camouflage military cap with a bill—the soldiers' uniform.

Oddly enough, Greg seemed nervous in the principal's office, more so than any child I had ever observed. He swung his legs rhythmically under the table and accidentally brushed my leg with one of his swings. He chewed on the end of his pen and tugged at his hat every few seconds. His incessant movements explained his wiry, muscular frame. He made me uncomfortable. But he was here to help us understand that Daniel was quite disturbed.

"Daniel likes attention," he explained. "I know that you've noticed that, Mrs. G. He'll do anything to get attention, even if it means getting in trouble on purpose and lying outright." Greg straightened himself in his chair as though he had just enlightened us with news we didn't already know. "I can't blame the kid, truth be told," he said. "His father was a drugged-out loser, his mother wants no part of him—and she's a piece of work, let me tell you. She practically *lives* at the casino. I have him because I married his mother and no one else seemed to want him. No grandparents, aunts, uncles. My parents had him when we were in Iraq. Quite frankly, I can't say that I'm wild about him and it's getting worse as he gets older. And now *this,* accusing me of beating him with a belt?"

Greg shook his head. I felt badly for him, living with a kid like Daniel who, despite being delightful in so many ways, was becoming a pathological liar.

Daniel complained of being hit by Greg a few more times, and we filed complaints with DCF for each one. He said that he was denied food, that no one would give him blankets when he was cold, and that Greg had locked him in the bathroom for hours. DCF was unable to substantiate what Daniel claimed—until one morning.

I arrived at my office and Daniel was sitting in the anteroom. Both his upper and lower lips were bloodied and swollen. His hands were smeared with what looked like old blood.

"Hi Mrs. G. I know I'm supposed to be in the cafeteria but I don't want anyone to see my face 'cause they'll laugh."

"What in the world happened to you?" I gasped.

"My stepfather punched me in the mouth because he said that I lied about where I was," he explained. "I was at Ryan's and I wasn't lying. He also grabbed my arm, right here, let me show you, so hard that he left marks." Daniel rolled up his sleeve and I could see the black and blue mark on his forearm.

"He also threw a cup of coffee at me, but the coffee wasn't that hot so I didn't get burned."

"Your hands are full of blood," I commented. "What's that from?"

"Probably my lips. I didn't wash them because I knew I needed evidence about him attacking me. No one ever believes me."

Daniel could have been punched and bruised by another kid, but I had a hunch that Daniel was telling the truth. Once again, I reported the abuse to DCF.

The next day, I received a phone call from the worker assigned to the case. Daniel was placed in a foster home until further notice based on substantiated child abuse, which, after further investigation, had been ongoing for quite some time.

A week later, Daniel came to school accompanied by his foster mother, a local woman named Donna Jane. She seemed like a kind person and Daniel said that he liked her so far. I spied a Bible on top of the pile of books he was carrying and asked him what he liked best about Donna Jane.

"I really like her food! She cooks everything: spaghetti and meatballs, fried chicken, beef stew! And she doesn't yell. I was getting sick of that!"

I called the teachers to see how Daniel was doing and everybody agreed that they were seeing improvement, aside from the teasing about his Bible toting. He seemed more comfortable and at ease.

I missed Daniel. He had become part of my routine. So I invited him to my office one day to ask about his own appraisal of how things were going at home and at school. I showed him my upgraded snack drawer: Kit Kat bars, Twizzles, Skittles. All the bad stuff.

"Do you want some Daniel? For old time's sake? To celebrate your new life?" I asked. I loved sharing snacks with Daniel.

"No thanks Mrs. G. I'm not really hungry right now, and I need to get going."

I wanted to hug him, kiss both of his chubby cheeks, but I could be fired for doing that.

"Are you sure? I'd like to chat about how things are going for you."

"No thanks, Mrs. G. Things are good for me now."

Indeed, they were. Daniel continued to stay in a foster home with people whom he could trust to provide him with good food, emotional support, and acceptance of his many quirks—all that he ever wanted. Greg, meanwhile, made no moves to get Daniel back home. Despite his original intentions to do right by Daniel and his brother, he realized in the end that he wasn't up to the job. In fact, he seemed to resent having the job all along if the investigative report is to be believed. After returning from Iraq, he found parenting to be more than he could handle, and that was when the abuse seemed to begin. Daniel had become collateral damage, the kind that the Department of Defense doesn't report.

BIG OLD TEDDY BEAR

M r. Steve Greeley applied to be a substitute teacher but found himself hired for Mrs. McMann's position instead. She had quit her job after teaching for five weeks in Room 37, the classroom for the behavior disordered kids.

Steve thought he got lucky that day. So did I.

I was the special education teacher in Mrs. McMann's classroom, and I was giddy with excitement because Steve was a big guy with a commanding presence. I sure didn't want to teach that crew alone. I prayed that having a man-mountain in the room, someone the kids would assume was the boss, would be a plus for me because these kids had few emotional or behavioral boundaries. Their placements in the classroom were testament to the powerlessness of general education teachers to manage them. Their behaviors rendered even the most competent of teachers into limp dishrags in a matter of weeks; hence the demise of the highly regarded Mrs. McMann.

It was difficult for anyone to fall in love with the 17 kids in that classroom. They were mostly boys, almost all of them diagnosed with ADHD. They were depressed, angry, unmotivated—with good reason. The student records told part of their sad stories—pages and pages filled with descriptions of failed marriages, broken child-parent relationships, and other fractured bonds which weighed them down like cement blocks at the bottom of a lake that was mucked up with algae and weeds. Many of these kids had been babies with FTT (failure to thrive), whose daddies were in jail, on parole, or on probation. Some lived with hapless grandmothers, ill equipped to deal with the children they had spawned, never mind the next generation. Drugs were the glue that knit this whole mess together—someone was either conspiring to use or sell, discreetly using or selling, or caught using or selling.

My giddiness and anticipation of Steve's ability to manage a classroom with this tough population morphed into disdain after just several weeks of co-teaching. Every day before my scheduled class time of 10:12, I worked hard to shed the blanket of dread that smothered me before I entered the classroom.

I'd sneak into the restroom for only a moment, close my eyes, and take some deep breaths—in and out, slowly. I'd visualize walking into a clean, organized classroom of typical eighth-graders seated at their desks, doing some last minute studying in preparation for class. The bell always interrupted my serenity-now moment, and I would trudge to Room 37, Steve's classroom, to find textbooks and half-finished handouts strewn under desks, in the middle of aisles, on bookshelves, basically on every available surface. Broken pencils and balled-up pieces of paper were scattered everywhere and the desks were arranged haphazardly. The kids roamed around aimlessly, like chickens scratching for feed. I might find a student yanking the glasses from someone's face or someone throwing an eraser at a girl's greasy-haired head. Kids would ball-up loose-leaf paper to use as basketballs for the wastebasket, which doubled as a makeshift hoop. The din reminded me of what I might hear at a crowded cocktail party following four hours of open bar, but the noise level still wasn't high enough to attract attention from the busy principal whose office was thirty yards down the hall.

Steve was typically stationed at his own disheveled desk when I arrived, his heavy, square head parallel to its surface, oblivious to the disorder around him. He pretended to be correcting papers, which I knew to be a ruse; few in that class took school seriously enough to produce anything that Steve needed to "correct." Steve rarely greeted me when I entered the room. I suppose this was his way of showing me that he was the lord of this particular manor, no matter how pathetic his fiefdom was.

By the time I would get the kids settled into their seats, I was already exhausted. Steve would remain seated at his desk, allowing me the daily pleasure of introducing structure and expectations (the first and only time of day when they existed). We were supposed to teach the writing class together, with me in the lead. However, this meant that I planned the lesson, that I prepared all the materials and that I introduced the lesson.

"I need your attention, now!" I'd say while walking the disordered aisles, straightening desks, and directing whomever to his proper seat. As I introduced bite-sized concepts that took less than five minutes to explain, I glanced at sad faces, masks of hopelessness and confusion. After modeling what was expected, I would give the students directions for their independent writing practice, which inevitably produced groans of protest.

Enter Steve. He would raise his massive frame from his desk chair, take a deep sigh, and stroll toward the nearest student, the reluctant savior of an unmanageable mob of lazy slugs. His imposing heft did quiet the grousing for a few minutes, but inevitably there would be manipulative shouts of, "This is too hard" and "I can't do this," or "I need help." I was too old and seasoned to be distracted by these cries for guidance that they didn't need.

I figured out early in our partnership that Steve might have been certified, but he didn't know how to teach. Or, he certainly didn't understand how to teach writing. He was the kind of teacher who "covered" material, but he could tell you neither what the students knew prior to his teaching nor how his teaching affected them. He just knew he had presented material, whether he was effective or ineffective was irrelevant. Steve didn't suggest ways in which the kids could improve their writing, nor did he point out parts of the model that students needed to use, never mind scoring against the rubric that I had meticulously developed. He told them all that their work was "good" and to "keep on working." Part of me didn't blame the kids for their apathy or unruliness. If I had spent most of the day with Steve and his half-hearted attempts at teaching, I would have been apathetic and unruly, or at least absent and surly.

One day after school, I mentioned my frustration with Steve to Kathy, a fellow teacher. I told her Steve was spiraling from apathy to unprofessionalism and neglect, and I was alarmed. I mentioned his recitation of jokes and limericks that made the kids so unfocused and riled up it would take over 15 minutes to settle them. I also confessed that he ridiculed my assignments out loud, yet he never discussed his dissatisfaction with me privately. But the worst was watching him throw pencils at kids who misbehaved, or calling his wife with orders for take-out and dry cleaning pick-up. My colleague listened intently to my concerns. "We're *not* on the same team," I said. "Like, he's actively trying to undermine me. For what reason, I can't tell you. I don't know if he feels inadequate or if just dislikes me. I'm not warm and fuzzy around him either, and he may be sensing that I am growing less and less fond of him. All I know is that something has to give or I'm going to have a heart attack from the stress."

"You'd never know it from what I've seen," said Kathy. "I've never seen Steve be disrespectful to anybody. He seems like a big, old teddy bear to me. He seems to really enjoy the kids, calling them nicknames and serenading them with rap songs every morning in the hallway. I never heard that he doesn't like you. Maybe you're too sensitive."

Kathy's words somewhat comforted me and I wanted to believe that he was not out to get me. It must be me, I thought. I don't like him and he knows it, so he doesn't like me. Should I ask to be transferred to another classroom? Should I ask for some mediation?

⇒‖⇐

Things didn't get much better in the weeks following my conversation with Kathy. I tried to smile more, give Steve a few compliments, and even ask for his input. But he just seemed to dig in more, as though he sensed my insincerity and that I was merely trying to make the best of a sorry situation. He knew I had little respect for him despite my pitiful overtures. I realized I had to have an honest discussion with Steve or approach my principal. I could sense my irritation growing day by day to the point where even something innocuous like a bathroom break I internalized as further evidence that he was a guileless oaf—stealing the

21

money of hard working taxpayers by doing a lousy job of educating their kids.

The week before Thanksgiving, I developed an assignment in which the kids were to write what they were thankful for by using compound and complex sentences. We had been working on these sentences for many weeks and they had to prove they could distinguish between the two. As I moved from student to student, so did Steve, repeating his usual refrain that the writing was good and to keep working. One student, Eric, approached me and softly read his essay aloud to me. It contained only simple sentences.

"Eric, this is a good essay but I'm sorry to say you didn't follow directions. Can you tell me what the assignment is?" Eric was one of the few students who was eager to please me and he looked ready to cry. He had been diagnosed with depression and his mood barely changed despite his medications. I hated doing this to him but I had to. He could do this work if he just knew what to do.

"Did I forget to give you the direction sheet?" I asked gently. It wasn't the end of the world but it looked as if it might be to him.

"Mr. Greeley told me it was good." he said quietly. "That's why I kept going."

Steve probably hadn't read the directions. Steve also hadn't read what Eric was writing. I was seething now. It was one thing to lead an unmotivated rascal astray, but quite another to mislead a kid like Eric who was desperate to prove that he could be successful. Eric was a perfectionist, ripping up papers that had only one mistake and forming his printed letters just so.

"You need to have compound and complex sentences Eric," I explained. "Here's another direction sheet. Just write your essay over and combine your sentences like we've been doing these last few weeks. I know you can do this! It'll be easy for you because your essay is all written!"

Despite my words of encouragement, Eric lowered his head and slowly plodded back to his desk. That was it. As soon as class was over, I waited for the last of the students to leave and then I went at Steve.

"Steve, I can't believe what you did today," I said. "You told Eric that his work was fine and it wasn't. I had to tell him to start all over again because he hadn't followed the directions. He was so disappointed! And frankly, so was I. I don't think you read the directions yourself and I don't think you even knew what the kids were supposed to be writing about. What kind of teacher are you anyway? I can't work in this mess of a classroom anymore. No order, no expectations. It's terrible."

I knew I was out of line and not handling myself well. "And why do you teach? I don't think you enjoy it at all! I think you just want an audience for your sick jokes and silly rapping. Maybe you should get a job where you can see your name in lights."

Steve's face reddened. There was no doubt in my mind that I'd made him stark raving mad. "Maybe you should stop prancing around here like you know everything, like you're the greatest teacher that ever walked the face of the earth," he said. "Sure, sure, you think you can teach, but can't you see that these kids don't give a shit? Maybe that's why *I* don't give a shit, either. You're in here one period a day and you get frustrated. I'm in here all day. Maybe *you* should try it, see if you feel all high and mighty at the end of the day." His fists were clenched and pressed into the sides of his thick thighs. He was doing his best to maintain some self-control, and I was suddenly mindful that he outweighed me by at least one hundred pounds. For the first time, I was scared of this man.

"Steve, we're both disappointed and frustrated. I apologize for what I said. I have to admit that some of it was unfair. I think it would be best if we slept on this and discussed our problems in a reasonable manner tomorrow."

Steve said nothing but his actions spoke louder than his words. He kicked a desk with such force that it landed on the floor and then stomped out of the classroom, slamming the heavy door as he exited. The intensity of Steve's rage scared but didn't surprise me. I knew he was passive aggressive. I had observed his calculated attempts to undermine my authority. But I had been passive aggressive as well. I had to admit that I made only half-hearted attempts to consult with him when planning or reviewing lessons. I should have tried to work harder with him. I knew that. But I honestly didn't respect Steve and I wanted no part of him.

⇥⇤

The next day, Steve refused to greet me in the hallway. When I went to his classroom, he stared at me and refused to work with the kids. He sat in his seat and glared. Some of the kids noticed and asked him why he was staring but he didn't answer. If he was trying to show that he was still the lord of the manor, he was doing a great job because I was starting to unravel. I later googled "workplace killers" thinking that I would surely become a victim. I even wondered if Steve would be apprehended and hauled off to jail to share a cell with some of the daddies of our students.

⊰⊹⊱

The staring went on for a week before I decided to tell the principal. I had hoped that Steve would soften and maybe I could find an opening to have the discussion I had proposed, but there was no change. Whenever I was in his classroom, I tried not to look his way and avoided going near his desk. I felt like a hunted beast that had to watch every move it made. I imagined him emerging suddenly from where he was sitting and grabbing me with his muscled arms to choke me to death. I wanted to sound calm when I relayed these fears to the principal, but inside I was a wreck. I didn't trust Steve's mental state and I began to search my memory for a time when he might have let it slip that he owned a gun or liked to dismember bodies.

I finally told Margaret, the principal of the school. She was not alarmed when I confessed my fear of Steve and described his behaviors. I told her about his teaching, his classroom management, anything to bolster my cause. "I'm afraid of Steve," I admitted. "I'm not joking." Margaret didn't try to dismiss my concerns. Her icy blue eyes softened and she nodded her head as I spoke. I wondered what she knew because she seemed so agreeable. I had visualized her peppering me with questions, challenging my thought processes, doing everything in her power to discredit my fears. Margaret had little tolerance for what she considered foolishness. The trick with her was figuring out what she considered foolish.

"You're not the first to complain about his bizarre behavior," she confessed. "A few other people have come to me, too. I've heard weird things. He stares at Dr. Marone during the literacy course he takes with her after school, and argues with her and I mean *loud* obnoxious arguing about grades he earns. Totally out of line. We told him yesterday that he's on probation and we drew up an improvement plan. Since he's been here less than 90 days, it'll be easy to get rid of him if we have to. Too bad we didn't know about your situation sooner. Anyway, I think he's out today, so he won't be doing any staring."

Her response did little to soothe me; I was still scared and worried about a workplace killing. I had three children at home who needed me.

From that day on, I eagerly scanned the morning's daily staff notice for news of Steve's absence, and each day I was heartened to hear that he was still out. This continued for six days, but in all this time he never called out sick. He just didn't show up. After the sixth day, the principal called Steve and told him to stay home forever. She informed him that his job was being given to someone else.

I didn't mind working with my third teacher in four months. The diminutive Mr. Howe and I got along just fine.

CALL IRENE

"Jordan McNally was the biggest challenge I've had in my twenty-one years in the classroom." This is what the fifth-grade special education teacher told me prior to Jordan's transition to the middle school. In my role as an administrator at the school, I had heard a lot about Jordan's behaviors, and I spent a good deal of time developing strategies to minimize their impact. Because Jordan wasn't able to speak, he often behaved aggressively when the staff couldn't discern what he wanted. I had to balance Jordan's need to be safe and the need for his rights to be protected. I also needed to assure that the rest of the kids were safe as well.

Jordan was almost twelve years old, with a vocabulary of one or two words. Despite the staff's best efforts to toilet train Jordan, he still urinated in his pants frequently (typically on his way to the restroom). Once, the staff left Jordan alone in a bathroom stall to tend to an emergency situation very close by, and he bolted down the sixth grade hall totally nude. I was thankful that there weren't any sixth-grade girls were in the hallway to spot him. I imagined a situation that could have generated hysterical phone calls from concerned parents and unfair recriminations for the staff.

The speech therapist tried to teach Jordan sign language and how to use an assistive technological device to speak, but his attention span was too short to master any meaningful words or phrases. He preferred to engage in repetitive behaviors like ripping up magazines or gazing at his hand when he spread his fingers in front of his face.

That Jordan was making little progress was no secret to the staff. He had severe cognitive impairments, and there was little hope that he would ever learn to read or write beyond a few words, if that. We focused on simple goals like toilet training and feeding himself.

The McNallys were not happy with the goals that his team of therapists and teachers developed for him. "He is capable of so much more," they said. They wanted him to talk and insisted that he receive additional speech therapy. They wanted him to work on pre-academic skills like matching shapes and colors in hopes that he would someday read. We were the realists and celebrated baby steps such as when Jordan held his built-up spoon for longer than one minute, pulled up his pants with verbal cues, or was redirected away from staring at his hand without a tantrum.

One afternoon, I received a phone call from Irene Picone, a crusty lawyer who had adopted a Korean child with severe special needs. I liked Irene. She was a straight shooter who didn't play games. Not everyone liked her rough-and-tumble approach though, especially my well-mannered principal.

"If it isn't the down-and-dirty and delightful Irene Picone," I said after she grunted hello.

"Don't go getting too friendly because you know I'm coming after you with both guns blazing," she said. "So, guess who's got me on their payroll? Give up? None other than Frank, the overbearing son-uv-a-bitch McNally, and his mousy wife Brenda. They want Jordan in another school because they say you people aren't doing much for him with that Erin what's-her-face, his teacher, yacking away on her cell phone all day, checking up on her kids or telling her hen-pecked husband to bring home some milk."

Whoa! That was a mouthful but not a surprise. The McNallys had started making noises during the last several months about placing Jordan at a private school, at the district's expense, of course. They were convinced that the problem was our staff and not Jordan's limitations. One thing they *were* right about was Erin using the phone all day while the aides did all the work. I had spoken to her many times about it but the principal didn't want to push any further because her father was a selectman in town.

"You still there?" Irene yelled after I took a few seconds to think. "They're saying they want a meeting. Pronto! Get this show on the road! Get a date for me! Time's a wastin'!"

'

"Irene, come on," I said. "You know Jordan is a very severe case. He's autistic and he's cognitively impaired. What is another school going to provide for him that we're not providing?"

"More one-on-one attention. More specialized care. You people aren't autism specialists. How do you know what he can do? He's the only one at his level that you guys have. The kid deserves better. So, you got a date?"

There was no use arguing with Irene.

"See you a week from Tuesday. Eleven o'clock."

"OK, kiddo," she said. "Get your team ready."

Kiddo? I was only three years younger than Irene.

As disappointed as I was about the McNallys' plans, I wondered if we were indeed underestimating Jordan. It wouldn't be the first time that I was wrong or the team was misguided. Still, I had enough experience to know that what our professional and clinical team had developed was certainly within the realm of best practice. Not to mention, spending fifty thousand dollars on an iffy proposition in a private school was going to add to the decimation of the special education budget that was currently en route to oblivion. This would mean less money for the rest of the kids in the school. Not fair, but very true.

The team met a few times to plan a strategy that would convince the McNallys that Jordan was getting the right training and to dissuade them from the private placement. Despite the team's preparations, I knew that they were nervous and intimidated by Irene.

On the day of the meeting, Mr. and Mrs. McNally showed up fifteen minutes early and requested a private meeting space so they could confer with Irene. I spotted them through the window as I walked to my office to pick up my notes. Mr. McNally was gesticulating with his arms while Irene rested her head in her hands, her elbows glued to the table. Irene did not look happy at all.

At 11 o'clock, everyone was seated around a large meeting table. Meetings like this drew a lot of players, and today there were twelve of us poised to make an argument for what we thought was best.

Mr. McNally asked me if he could speak first, given that he was the parent and he had called the meeting. After we had all introduced ourselves, I signaled him to begin. I imagined myself in Mrs. McNally's place as Mr. McNally began to speak. Here she was, seated in a room full of people who were doing their jobs, fighting as hard as she could for the one person in the world who was on the earth because of her, because she wanted him more than anything she ever wanted in my life. Looking at this mother and father made me want to cry. And I also had a flashback to my own mother, a moment I will never forget.

My mother was looking out of the window in our family room. In all my eighteen years of living with her, I had never seen her stare outside like this. She was unusually quiet for what seemed like hours but it was really only a few minutes when she finally said, "Jerry is playing outside." Jerry Marchand was seven years old. He was small for his age and was sitting in a pile of leaves in his fenced backyard which was next door to ours. He gathered some leaves and lifted them over his head. He raised his face toward the sun so that the leaves fluttered onto his face as they descended toward the ground. Jerry laughed and repeated this over and over again. Beneath his corduroy overalls, Jerry wore a diaper. He also could not speak. His skin was pasty white and he had been walking independently for only a few years. I heard Jerry's mother, Clare, call him for lunch, but he just continued to lift the leaves, drop the leaves, and laugh when they kissed his face. "When Robbie died, I think I was the lucky one," my mother said. "Clare will have heartache for the rest of her life." Robbie, my brother, her son, had died of cancer three months earlier. He was in the seventh grade.

Mr. McNally's booming voice jettisoned me back to reality. He was not an attractive man and I wondered what Brenda saw in him. She was petite, stylish and well coiffed, obviously very concerned about appearances. Mr. McNally's face was pockmarked from the scourge of adolescent acne, and what little hair he had was slicked back. His grey suit looked tailored and expensive.

Mr. McNally's eyes swept the room, scrutinizing each of us. Irene seemed to be holding her breath. She clearly was not pleased.

"Now, everyone, before I *truly* begin, I want to say that I am not accustomed to speaking to people like you, people who work in schools. I travel all over the world due to my position with Intel, the company that has employed me for the last 18-and-a-half years. Typically, I speak with high level executives about very high level ideas and plans, so you'll excuse me as I try to speak at a different level than what I am used to."

Irene lowered her head, shaking it from side to side. The rest of us sat expressionless.

"My son Jordan, as you all know, has been in this school for almost one whole school year, and quite frankly, my wife and I are very disappointed at the lack of progress that we've seen. If anything, Jordan has regressed. I know, I know, you'll say that he is approaching adolescence and his aggression is escalating due to his rising levels of male hormones. He should be making significantly more progress according to Dr. Yancy, a world-renowned autism specialist whom I'm sure none of you have ever heard of. From what my wife and I can gather, most of you are clueless about autism and I will *not* allow my son to be the victim of your ignorance."

Irene was incensed. "Listen here, Frank," she shouted. "I told you before we came into this meeting that if you were going to insult the people in this room, I would refuse to be your advocate. I stand by my word and you know I do. You are incredibly inappropriate right now and I am telling you to sit down, shut up, and let me do the talking. And if what I'm saying to your incredibly rude self doesn't sit well with you, then I quit and you are on your own. Capiche?"

I looked at my hands because I didn't know where else to look. My colleagues shifted in their seats, embarrassed by Irene's outburst, but like me, secretly pleased that she had put the bully in his place.

"Now, you go on back to that highfalutin office of yours at Intel or wherever the hell you work, and let me deal with these good people," she continued. "I know them to be more than reasonable and I can assure you that everyone in this room will do what's best for Jordan. And you can take that to the bank!"

Mr. McNally, clearly unnerved, gathered his papers. "Let's go," he said to his wife, who scurried to get out of her chair and head for the door. "Let Irene handle it since she seems to believe that I'm some kind of a buffoon!" He slammed the door.

"*OK!*" Irene said. "So where were we?"

It seemed like even the walls had breathed a sigh of relief, and we got on with the meeting. Irene methodically worked through her stack and cited data from the teachers and the clinicians to prove her point that Jordan was not benefitting from the training that he was receiving. She cited lapses in our judgments which she backed with opinions from local autism professionals. Although I thought we had done a good job of providing facts to support Jordan's continued placement in our school, it was clear that Irene had done a better job of demonstrating that he would do better in the school that the McNallys had chosen.

There was no denying that Irene was a very good advocate. There were times when I was witness to Irene advising parents to back off when they made demands on behalf of their children that were unreasonable. She told parents when she thought the schools were doing a wonderful job and coached them on how to be effective when communicating with school personnel. Parents could rely on Irene to do what was ethical, legal and justified.

Jordan ended up in the expensive private school where he belonged. Irene had made her case and I respected her because of it. And Jordan got what he so desperately needed.

When people ask me to recommend a good advocate for their children, I always say, without hesitation, "Call Irene."

CAN YOU IMAGINE WHAT IT'S LIKE?

Rumors circulated almost immediately about Mi-Cha Choi and the circumstances surrounding her arrival in town. People said that her parents had been brought here to the U.S. against their will and worked as slaves for a wealthy Indian couple. They said that the parents weren't allowed out of their "master's house" because the Indian couple were afraid there would be trouble with the police.

Donna, a math teacher in our school, complained to me often about the new Korean seventh grader who refused to speak. "The kid just stares at me when I speak to her," she told me. "No expression on her face, no acknowledgement that I am even speaking. It's like talking to one of those characters in a wax museum. What am I supposed to do with her? She's a big lump in my class! I hate to sound mean, but it's true. Can you test her? Figure out what the story is? I know that there is something very wrong with this kid."

The teachers in this suburban middle class school weren't accustomed to dealing with immigrant kids, but I was. I knew that some children don't even try to speak English within the first six months of their arrival. Mi-Cha was not that different from kids I had seen over the course of my teaching career. True, I hadn't dealt with Korean children. Maybe the couple had told Mi-Cha to keep quiet, not to talk.

We had little reason to suspect that anything was amiss at home. Mi-Cha was certainly well dressed and well nourished. In fact, she was a bit overweight. Her attendance was good, and there was no physical evidence of anything that would suggest abuse or neglect. All we had were rumors and Mi-Cha's prolonged silence.

A year went by and not much changed with Mi-Cha. I was beginning to think that Donna was right. Eighth-grade teachers began to complain about Mi-Cha's stony silence, the blank look on her face, and her unwillingness to complete the simplest of watered-down assignments. Lisa, an ESL teacher, stopped me in the hallway one day in December to talk about her charge. "I'm getting nowhere with Mi-Cha," she explained. "A-year-and-a half and we're still working on the alphabet, basic words, and directions. I know that she won't talk to anyone, but at this point she should be way past that phase. I get that she must be overwhelmed, but my sense is that she's depressed or something. This behavior is not normal and we need to figure out what the problem is before she goes to high school. If she *can* go to high school, because in no way will she be able to function without the cocoon of this middle school. She's not making progress and we need to know why."

I knew Lisa was right. I also knew that I needed a Korean school psychologist who could test in Korean with a Korean testing kit, and who could interpret the results in English. Did this person even exist in New England? What was that going to cost the system? We were already way over budget for special education costs.

Meanwhile, I observed Mi-Cha in the cafeteria, in the halls between classes, waiting for the bus to take her to her alleged "prison" after the bell rang. She always walked with her eyes glued to the floor, clutching her books closely to her chest. When kids said hello to her, she responded with a tight smile to show her appreciation but offered nothing else. I began to think that her real prison was our school. After watching her behavior for weeks, I realized that we had to help this poor kid, whatever the cost. I became obsessed with trying to locate a Korean school psychologist. I was ready to give up when I finally spoke to someone who was a member of a Korean Presbyterian Church who knew someone who might know someone. Bingo! This someone had a test kit! She spoke Korean and could test in Korean! And she charged three thousand dollars!

Sook-Joo Kim was a native Korean who was finishing her doctorate at the University of Connecticut and was headed to Hawaii in a couple of weeks. "No time to waste," she informed me.

⤜╬╬⤛

Sook-Joo finished the test and her report three days before her scheduled departure. I called a meeting with the eighth-grade team and Mi-Cha's parents to discuss the results and recommendations. I had been given no hint of what Sook-Joo was planning to say.

Mi-Cha's parents arrived to the meeting with their own interpreter, even though I had hired one for the meeting. Her parents were short and compact in stature like Mi-Cha and barely made eye contact with the teachers upon introduction. I knew it was far-fetched, but I wondered if this interpreter had been sent by the Indian couple to ensure the parents didn't tip us off about their circumstances. As chairperson, I insisted that the school interpreter would be the official interpreter so we could be assured of accuracy.

The meeting began with the teachers' assessments of Mi-Cha's academic performance. The litany of complaints varied little from teacher to teacher. "There was nothing new." "Silence." "Selective mutism, perhaps," one teacher suggested. "No engagement with assignments." "A sad look." "Doesn't socialize." "Like talking to a brick wall." Several teachers proposed that Mi-Cha's behavior was defiant and willful, and that she was merely lazy and entitled. I resented some of these remarks. What I had seen with Mi-Cha was a child struggling to make sense of a very different culture.

Finally, it was Sook-Joo's turn to read her report. She read her scores on achievement tests and cognitive tests and ended with her recommendations for how to proceed. "Mi-Cha has border-line average intelligence. I saw a few discrepancies in her cognitive abilities, and I could make the case for a learning disability that would get her some special education services. This team will have to decide on this, of course. What I was more concerned about was Mi-Cha's emotional status. How this emotional condition was impacting her learning seemed clear to me, but I knew we could run into some difficulty because, once again, the diagnosis of depression wasn't clear-cut. Mi-Cha does not present with the characteristics you are all describing at home."

Sook-Joo's report also included a synopsis of a home visit. Mrs. Choi said that Mi-Cha was cheerful and chatty at home. She reported that she ate well and slept well with no social difficulties when she was with other Koreans. The parents told Sook-Joo that Mi-Cha had been a good student in Korea with lots of friends. Sook-Joo explained her findings to the parents and they nodded as though they understood. The Chois were very surprised at what the school was reporting.

"The parents," the interpreter said, "are also confused about some long distance phone calls that are appearing on their phone bill. And Mi-Cha admitted that she called her aunt in Seoul several times, begging for her help to return to Korea. She even tried to make secret plans with her aunt to run away. She made her aunt promise not to tell or she would kill herself. When the parents questioned Mi-Cha about the calls and the threats, she admitted that the aunt was telling the truth."

"Why is Mi-Cha so unhappy here?" I asked. "Can you shed a little light on this? From what I can see, we've all worked pretty hard to help her in our school."

"Well, maybe most of your staff has, but not all," explained Sook-Joo. "You need to understand Korean culture to get what's going on here. For the most part, it is a shame-based culture, as are other Asian cultures. Saving face is very important, as is pleasing people in authority. In Korean schools, when someone is a slow learner or perceived as not conforming to group expectations, she is ridiculed, physically attacked by the teachers, and placed in the back of the room where she is ignored until she conforms. For some kids, sitting in the back and being ignored is how they spend all of their school years."

"Now picture this," Sook-Joo said. "You come to a new country where you can't even recognize the alphabet, the building block of the whole learning system, and you don't understand anything that anyone is talking about. Your school experience tells you that if anyone catches on that you know nothing, you will be banished to no man's land. You can't very well discuss this with your parents, because you don't want to embarrass them. You're frightened about what's going to happen to you. No one speaks your language except your uncle who helped you to get here. Can you imagine what it's like for a young girl like Mi-Cha? This is the stuff that your fiction is made of, but this is her reality."

Mi-Cha's mother said she wanted to address the group and the interpreter asked me for permission to translate what she had to say. I nodded.

"I am sorry for the trouble my daughter has caused in this school," she began. "We came to America so she can have opportunities, not to be problems for anyone. My daughter, I know now, is very unhappy here, and I want her to be happy like she was in Korea. A happy, popular girl who worked hard. She needs to work hard to get ahead. She can't get ahead in Korea like she can here. That's why we came. Please help my daughter."

"Thank you, Mrs. Choi. We want to help your daughter," I said. This situation was heart wrenching. This poor kid had no one who could understand her difficulties, and had even considered suicide if she was exposed. I was determined to make this situation right and I didn't care what it took to do so. "I'd like to make a suggestion to this team," I added. "Let's say that Mi-Cha has some learning disabilities and depression, even if we're not totally sure, so we can get the extra services she needs. I know, I know, it's not totally kosher, but let's do it anyway. We can make a case for it, maybe not a strong case, but any sane person who examines this situation will see that it makes sense. And let's have Mi-Cha repeat eighth grade to give her more time to prepare for high school. And finally, can we adjust our expectations and attitudes to reflect that we are dealing with a child who is suffering in a way that not one of us has ever experienced? Can we acknowledge that we have learned an important lesson today?"

"I'll be happy to stay with Mi-Cha for extra help after school," offered one of the two teachers present. "I will as well," said the other. "Mi-Cha needs to get ready for high school. Thank you to Ms. Kim for helping us to understand what was so baffling. Now that we get it, I'm sure we can move forward with Mi-Cha."

An apology of sorts.

I knew these two educators would do their best by Mi-Cha now that the truth was out.

⇒⊦⊦⇐

Mi-Cha received special education services and repeated eighth grade. She moved on to the high school and performed well enough to graduate. In the end, what helped Mi-Cha the most was the acceptance and understanding from the whole staff.

If you want to change the behavior of others, change your own behavior first.

"DO *YOU* HAVE CHILDREN?"

Jimmy, the school's crisis intervention specialist, told me about a new student coming from the Bennington School, and what he told me did not make me happy.

Ramon, a seventh grader, was apprehended while carrying a knife that had a ten-inch blade. This was the third time that Ramon had been caught with a knife; only this time the blade was four inches longer.

The Bennington was a large school set in the midst of a drug-ridden, decaying neighborhood, and the administrators there certainly didn't want this child in their school. By comparison, our school was quite small with only one class in each grade. Jimmy said that Ramon would have less potential for finding victims to bully (or supporters to join in) if he were with us. Presumably, the teachers in our school would be able to monitor him more closely. However, despite the fact that Ramon presented as dangerous and emotionally disturbed, the talk was that his mother didn't want him placed in a school for kids like himself. He had special needs and she knew that the school system had to "prove" it couldn't accommodate him before he was outplaced.

Fifteen minutes after receiving Jimmy's report, a notice from the principal arrived letting us know that Ramon and his mother, who was dressed in a business suit, were on their way to my class.

Ramon had finely-chiseled features and looked to be sixteen years old. He had the physique of a grown man and was very broad shouldered for a boy who was not yet thirteen years old. His kinky hair was tightly cropped. He wore a navy-blue-and-gold Ralph Lauren jacket with the collar turned up—the model son and student.

I introduced Iris, his soon-to-be instructional aide, and myself. His mother introduced herself and her son and said she was grateful that we were taking Ramon as a student and hoping that he would settle in nicely.

"This classroom certainly looks like what the doctor ordered for my Ramon, so cheery and welcoming. Right Ramie?"

Ramon stared straight ahead, expressionless. "If you say so," he finally mumbled.

"Oh, I'll show Ramon around and get him settled with supplies and a schedule and he'll be just fine," I lied. I felt compelled to say something to help this poor woman feel more at ease. Her lovely face was pinched with pain.

⇒┼┼⇒

I was on edge for the first few days, waiting for an emotional outburst or some type of altercation that I was unprepared for. Ramon was on his best behavior, but I wondered where the real Ramon was hiding. Jimmy had brought me his school records that included rather unflattering teacher comments. The more I read, the more apprehensive I became. I told Jimmy to come by often, just to make sure that Ramon hadn't taken the rest of us hostage. He thought I was joking. I wasn't.

My worst problem in that first week was figuring out how to manage Maria, the eighth grader who had fallen in love with Ramon and his jacket, that first day he strolled into class. But by the start of the second week, my problems worsened. Ramon started bragging about having a knife, saying he had been stabbed in the chest the year before.

"Yeah right!" Maria scoffed.

"I was stabbed last year," Ramon insisted.

I could see his face reddening; it was obvious that he was not used to being challenged. "I'll show you, you dumb ass," he said.

He removed his jacket, pulled his T-shirt over his head, and sure enough there was a four-inch scar on his chest. "See, I wasn't kidding."

The other students were impressed. "Wow," said Yonaton. "You need a knife to protect yourself all right!"

"I was eleven when I got this," Ramon bragged.

Ramon was too savvy for these younger ones.

"Please pull your T-shirt down and quit the knife talk," I ordered.

On the heels of a trying week, including a playground melee with Ramon the ringleader, we arranged for a meeting with Ramon's special education team and mother, who announced she would be bringing a lawyer.

The meeting began with a synopsis of what we had observed in the two weeks of Ramon's stay—that he seemed to derive little academic and social benefit from the school. But, the lawyer disagreed, insisting that Ramon loved the classroom and how safe he felt there.

"Well, the rest of us feel unsafe with him," I said. "And besides, what is it about this school that he loves so much?"

There was silence. But we all knew the answer. Ramon liked being the head rat in a nest full of helpless mice.

Ramon's mother didn't speak, perhaps embarrassed by her son and the havoc he had generated. I felt badly for her. She had a lot going against her. She had no husband and little support.

"Ramon has been through a lot," she said finally, dabbing at her teary eyes. "His sister died in a fire last year and he is upset that he couldn't save her. Kids picked on him a lot in the projects and that's why he always wants to have a knife. I had him in counseling but it didn't seem to do any good. He went, but he just sat there, never said anything. The therapist said that maybe we should find someone else. I don't know what to do with this kid. I have to work. I can't watch him after school and that's when he gets into all his trouble. Don't tell me he should go to the Boys' Club. He won't go. Honestly, he's taken over my household. He's become the boss and I do what he tells me to do. It's sick and I know it. It's really sick."

Her story was heart wrenching and we all nodded our heads in agreement.

Even so, I had to focus on what was best for my students, not just for Ramon. The discussion went around in circles, first blaming Ramon, then sympathizing with his mother, then throwing up our hands at the lack of solutions.

"Can I say something, as the teacher in the classroom that has been totally disrupted by the arrival of Ramon?" I said, turning to the lawyer, who was the main provocateur in my view, and determined to keep Ramon in my classroom.

"Do you have children?" I asked.

"Yes, I do," he said.

"Boys? Girls? How old?"

"Two boys, eight and eleven."

"Same ages as my boys," I said. "Let me ask you something then. Would you like your precious boys in a classroom with Ramon?"

The lawyer didn't say anything.

"I am guessing not," I said. "And you know what? I wouldn't want my boys in a classroom with him either. So why is it OK for parents of the nine and ten year olds in my classroom to have Ramon with their kids? You wouldn't tolerate this for your kids and neither would I."

"I really have no answer for you," he said, shaking his head. "I think you're right and we need to find another place for Ramon. This isn't the place. I know that. We were just trying to buy time for him, and I see now, at your expense."

I had won this round, at least. I was elated.

He looked over at Ramon's mother. "Agree?"

She nodded and said, "I know that everyone is doing their best but I don't want my Ramon to be intimidating little kids, which is what I think you're telling me is going on. He belongs with big boys like himself."

The lawyer gathered his papers. "We'll look for another place for Ramon. It'll take a few weeks, but you'll be hearing from us."

The victory was bittersweet. I was pleased that Ramon would be going to a place more suited to his needs, but the words I spoke to that lawyer weighed on me for days. The team had gathered in that meeting for almost an hour, and if I hadn't spoken up, Ramon would have been in my classroom until the end of the school year. Why did we even entertain the idea that it might be OK for young Hispanic kids to tolerate junior criminals in a classroom?

When I was an eighth grader, my teacher, Sister Catherine, once wrote a quote on the chalkboard that has motivated me so many times in my life, including this time. It read, *If not you, then who?*

"I DIDN'T SEE A THING"

My favorite part of the school day was when the dismissal bell rang and most kids and teachers had scurried out with the dismissal bell. I always had a lot of planning to do for the next day and I basked in the solitude. But I didn't like being completely alone in the building. And I wasn't.

Richie, our new twenty-nine-year-old custodian, was responsible for cleaning and maintaining the decrepit brick building we called a school. Impressive in its heyday in the early 1920's, the building now reeked of neglect and obsolescence. Sadly, there was no gymnasium, no library and it was filthy. I felt badly whenever I watched Richie battle the decades-old grime. Like all of the custodians before him, Richie was an immigrant who was clawing his way to a better life, and like his predecessors, Richie took pride in his work. I liked that about him.

Occasionally, I heard Richie in the office across from my classroom speaking in Spanish on the phone to Rosita, his wife who worked at town hall. *Si mi amor,* he would say. He often poked his head into my classroom to say hello, or to ask if I needed anything moved or fixed. I rarely did. He would lean against his broom as he chatted about his young daughters, Jamie and Heather. "Yes, American names," he said with pride. Richie liked gossiping with me about lazy people, especially other custodians who took long breaks, and about teachers who left classrooms filled with balled-up pieces of paper and broken pencils. I usually didn't have a lot of time to gossip, and sometimes I would get impatient as he rambled on and on, but I hated to cut him off; I knew I was probably the only person he could chat with during his shift. Our daily bantering had nurtured a friendship of sorts.

One Indian summer afternoon, I opened my classroom window. Outside was a racket of screeching tires and slamming car doors, and I immediately tried to shut out the noise by closing the window, but the temperamental window jammed in the runner. I tried to jimmy and wiggle it, but nothing worked.

I shouted out to Richie in the hallway, "Richie, can you help me with this window, it's stuck."

"Sure, sure!" he yelled back. "For you, anything."

He smiled as he entered the classroom, and then lifted his eyebrow. I chuckled. I knew he wanted permission before grabbing a piece of wrapped chocolate from the jar that sat on the bookcase.

"Sure, Richie," I said. "For you, anything! Take all you want."

He popped a piece of chocolate in his mouth and began to coax the window back into its frame, but something caught his eye. "Oh no," he said, pointing out the window.

"What? What?" I said hurrying to see. Maybe Richie was watching a drug deal go down or a raging pit bull. I had seen worse outside that window.

"Oh no," he repeated. "I just saw Desiree go through the back door. I thought that I had locked that door so no one could get in. I can't stand that kid and I ain't supposed to let anyone in the building after hours. She's gonna steal whatever she can get her hands on."

Richie rushed out of the classroom. Desiree was one of those kids that even the social workers and counselors didn't like. In any school, there are a few children that most teachers dislike, but there is always some adult who will defend them and find some redeeming quality. But Desiree had no takers. She called teachers by their first names, and if she didn't like what they were saying, she would pound on her desk until the teacher stopped talking. When chastised, she put her fingers in her ears, squeezed her eyes shut, and stuck out her tongue. Her untamed verbiage got her enrolled in plenty of afternoon detentions and in-house suspensions, but there was little change.

An earsplitting crash echoed down the hallway, and I bolted from my desk to see what was going on. It sounded as if a metal supply cabinet had toppled to the floor.

"Get your fucking hands *offa* me, you lowlife!" Desiree screeched

"Shut up, shut up, you no good little whore! Just shut the fuck up and get the hell out of here!"

I had never heard Richie swear, never mind talk like this.

Desiree certainly didn't deserve to be assaulted. I had a flashback to a time when I had been accosted for much less.

I was in the first grade at St. Marguerite's School. It was raining too hard for outside recess, and Sister Lidwin instructed us to walk around the cafeteria for fifteen minutes instead. Sister said that we needed to walk in a straight line and remain perfectly silent. I lowered my head but stared at her through upturned eyes. Sister was a little taller than I, a tiny person that my cousin in the fifth grade called Thumbelina.

It was hard not to talk for fifteen minutes while walking, walking, walking. My neighborhood pal, David was behind me, and I knew he would talk to me if I talked to him. I was so bored.

"Do you think this is fun? I don't."

I didn't see Sister Lidwin headed my way, but I sure could feel her smack my bottom over and over and over, as though once wasn't enough. I whipped around to apologize. But I couldn't tear my gaze from her bushy eyebrows that had grown together at the top of her nose. She glared at me for several seconds before she spoke: "You turn around, young lady. Be quiet! No talking, I said! This isn't outside recess! This is indoor recess and during indoor recess, no one talks!"

My eyes watered but I didn't want the other kids to see me cry. Sister Lidwin's face was blurry and all I could see was that white piece of cardboard her veil was sewed onto. It dug into her forehead creating a little ridge of fat that ran parallel to those thick eyebrows.

"Do you understand, Miss Beaulieu? Do. You. Understand?" No, I wanted to say. No, I do not understand at all. I loved Sister Lidwin, and I always thought that she loved me, too. I didn't understand. If you loved someone, why did you hit her? If you didn't love someone, then you could hit her I guess. Did she hate me? Is that what adults did when they were angry? Hit people?"

I looked down the hallway and saw Richie. His large hand was pressed against Desiree's chest, right between her small breasts. She was unable to move, although she did try to wiggle her way out of his clutch. Her wiggling only strengthened his resolve to keep her pinned against the wall. His nose was only five inches away from hers and his shoulders were heaving while he stared into her eyes with a wild determination.

"Richie!" I screamed in horror. Take your hands off of her. Right now!"

"Why? You tell me why," Richie demanded. "She knocked the cabinet down and when I tried to grab her, she slapped me 'cross the face! She ain't going nowhere 'til she apologizes!"

"And that ain't going to happen, plus, your breath stinks, you spic." Desiree jutted out her chin and spat square in Richie's face.

I saw Richie stiffen. It wasn't a large amount of spit, but there was enough for it to gather momentum and begin to roll down his cheek. He raised his right arm, wiped the spit away with his sleeve, and then he pulled his arm back. In one swift motion he slapped Desiree across her cheek.

Desiree let out a loud yelp like an animal whose leg had just been snared in a trap. Her cheek was red and she looked like she might cry.

I stared, stunned, watching Richie's rage consume him. I lunged toward him in a panic.

"Richie, you're out of control. Get away from her. Let her go." I tried to yank his hand from her chest. I am not a strong person, but my own rage seemed to fuel whatever strength I was able to muster. I couldn't get his hand away, so I pulled at his shirt and he released his grip. Desiree escaped down the hallway.

"Go on home, asshole," Richie hollered after her.

He leaned against the wall of the hallway, looking up at the ceiling. His breath was shallow and uneven. His black hair hung in wet ringlets down the back of his neck.

"Richie, what the hell happened? What got into you? I've never seen you lose your cool like that. My God, you're an employee in a school. Are you crazy?"

"No, I ain't crazy. She went straight to her classroom and I caught her pullin' the drawers out from the desk, throwin' stuff on the floor, lookin' for money. I yelled, 'Stop!' and that's when she ran here and pushed the cabinet down. Tryin' to get away from me."

"You are in big trouble. You know that don't you?" I said this as much to myself as to him. It was obvious that this needed to be reported. Richie would lose his job for sure. Then what would he do? His life would be ruined.

"That's *if* anyone finds out," Richie schemed. "You think Desiree will tell anyone? Who would believe her, the way she lies all the time. Where's the proof? Her word against mine? Ha! Slammed her like I did. Lotta people around here are wantin' to do it to her. All you people tiptoe around her like you're afraid of her, and you know it. Looks like I'm the first to show that little whore who's boss!" Richie sounded almost proud.

I gasped at his boastfulness. "Frankly, Richie, I'm torn here. You did wrong. Very wrong. You're guilty of assault and battery. Of a minor no less!"

"Yes, but she deserved it, you know she deserved it," he said. "Don't turn me in. Please! I'll never get another job. If you turn me in, I'm done. My whole family is done. What? You're tellin' me that if someone spit in your face, you'd let him get away with it? Yeah right." Richie's bottom lip began to quiver and he turned around to face the wall. His put his arm over his eyes to shield his tears. "What the hell," he said sounding defeated. "I ain't got a chance in this city with all the prejudice around here. People calling me spic and hatin' on me for no reason. I'm no pimp and no drug dealer. I'm a good dad to my kids even though I ain't never had no father myself. I work hard every day, coming in here, doing my best, helpin' you teachers. You see me every day. You know I do. Maybe, if you don't say anything, no one will know."

"Richie," I said, "you did the wrong thing. You can't go slapping kids who you think are stealing, or who break furniture or spit at you. Or swear. Or pound desks. We have procedures to handle that." Well, we had procedures all right, but they didn't work...or we didn't implement them.

As I talked about Desiree's behaviors, I felt myself softening, as though her despicable behaviors, reviewed as a whole, could mitigate some of the damage of Richie's heinous reaction. Richie was right, of course. We were afraid of Desiree and we had let her do what she wanted, when she wanted. We had all grown tired of trying to rein her in, to give her boundaries. She had outwitted all of us. Desiree deserved Richie, someone who would finally put her in her place. Desiree would feel no shame as I had when I was a young girl, even though I had done so little to deserve being smacked like I was. I wanted Desiree to know adults warranted respect. School warranted respect. She had never received that message, so maybe Richie's outburst was a lesson she could understand—that there were some people you just can't mess with. A valuable lesson for sure.

Richie looked at me sheepishly. "Look, I'm sorry. I'm sorry. I mean it. Help me, Mona! Desiree doesn't even know what I did was wrong. That's how screwed up the kid is. I was wrong. I know it. But I can't lose my job over it."

I knew he was right. I had to stick by him.

"Richie," I said. "I never saw a thing."

EL JEFE

The seventh-grade classroom was always in disarray when I arrived to teach writing at ten o'clock. The three large wastebaskets overflowed with torn pieces of paper and broken pencils were scattered everywhere like peanut shells after a ball game. Desks and chairs were always overturned and students wandered aimlessly. Every day I had to force myself to twist that classroom's doorknob, pull the door open, and fight the urge to cut and run as I walked into pure chaos.

Steve was the lead teacher who I had suspected was hired to contain—not teach—this class of seventeen "behavior disordered" students. Why? Because Steve was so big, few students would mess with him. And what the six-foot-seven-inch Steve lacked in teaching ability and classroom management skills, he made up for with ample girth and slothful disengagement. Not wanting to waste what little energy he had, Steve conducted the class while seated at his expansive desk that was squeezed into a corner of the room.

I hated the 47 minutes I had to spend with him and the students.

I typically enjoyed teaching but this crew sapped every ounce of energy. By the end of my lesson, I felt as if I had spent 70 hours engaged in non-stop negotiations with the policemen's union. I didn't blame the kids for taking advantage of no lesson plans, no rules, no expectations. I was angry with Steve for creating this mess.

I knew I had to change these conditions if only for the short time that I was in the room every day. If I wanted them to learn to write, I had to be able to teach. In this den of messy depravity, I needed to establish some authority and a sense of order.

After several months, I managed to get everyone seated, with nothing on their desks but what was needed for the assignment—no squishy toys, candy, Gatorade, rubber bands. My new rules didn't make me popular, and some kids actually groaned when I entered the room. They didn't like sitting in their desk chairs and listening to directions. I sensed that Steve was resentful of the new order because he would lift his head, stare, and then give me a dismissive glance. He rarely bothered to stir from his perch to assist.

I usually began a lesson by outlining my behavioral expectations in fifty words or less—few kids had the attention span to listen any longer than that. The directions for the writing assignment were mounted on chart paper, and I reviewed them with the students. Finally, I would distribute the materials that the students needed so that they didn't waste time looking for their own or making up excuses for why they didn't have their pens. When everyone had what was needed, I visited with each student, offering assistance with his or her first draft, and final drafts. I'd sit beside the students, coaching, coaxing, chiding, whatever was necessary to get results. The Hispanic kids began to call me *El Jefe* or "The General." I was proud that we had established some sense of order, at last.

≔╬≕

Kenny was a new student who enrolled in the first weeks after I established myself as El Jefe. He was quiet and spoke very little. I knew he was severely dyslexic, and before he began his first assignment I sat down next to him to help. I took off my glasses and placed them on his desk.

"Let me help you get started," I said.

He slipped me a coy side-eye then snatched my glasses, put them on, and strolled to the front of the room. This was so bizarre, but instead of directing him to get back in his chair, I just watched, speechless.

He clapped his hands twice, then three times repeatedly, which got the attention of everyone. "Listen up!" Kenny commanded. "I want nothing on the desk! No-thing! No food, no drinks, no books! Just what I give you! No one goes to the bathroom or gets a drink until I'm gone! Don't ask! The answer is no!"

He was mocking me—the pitch of my voice, the inflection, the emphasis on certain words. It was perfect and I burst out laughing. The kid was hilarious.

Once the other students saw my reaction, they all joined in, encouraging Kenny, of course, to continue his stand-up. "Before you begin, make sure you read the directions again. Don't be bothering me with questions when the answer is right in front of you."

The kids howled.

"No gum. You know better than that. And don't forget to put your name on your paper. No name, no mahk." Kenny had my Boston accent down with aplomb. "Do your own work. Anyone caught cheating gets a zero!"

He looked over his glasses at Nomar, "Settle down, Nomar. Save the nonsense for after school."

Now the class was in hysterics, and the kids chanted, "Ke-nny! Ke-nny! Ke-nny!"

Kenny took my glasses off and handed them back to me. He sat back down at his desk. He turned to face his classmates, and held his open hand up to indicate that it was time for the laughter to stop. "Enough!" he said.

I barely knew what his voice had sounded like because he had rarely said anything. And here he was, entertaining all of us, even me, with complete mastery of his subject. I realized that I was experiencing an "Aha" moment. The kids sensed that the real me was not El Jefe, despite all my posturing to the contrary. I was a phony general, a leader who preferred a relaxed atmosphere. I suppose I should have been angry given the disruption, but I loved laughing at myself with the kids and it was a bonding moment, as though we now shared an inside joke.

"Kenny, that was masterful," I said. "You showed that you pay attention to detail and that's a great skill for a writer to have."

"Ms. G, you're not mad?" one of the students asked.

I slid my glasses down my nose and nodded my head forward so I could look over them. "No, I actually got a kick out of it. But let's settle down and save any more nonsense for after school."

"FREE EDWIN MELENDEZ!"

E dwin Melendez was one of the first students I met when I began my second teaching job. He was one of those unfortunate kids who had some intellectual heft but no adult to guide its trajectory. Teachers who knew him in the earlier grades said Edwin had been a bully for years. By the time he reached the eighth grade, Edwin had perfected his persona as a loner and an outcast. There was accordance among the teachers that he was the alpha wolf at the top of the eighth grade food chain, always stalking for prey.

It certainly wasn't his physique that all of us found intimidating. Edwin was lean, maybe even somewhat underweight, and about five feet seven inches tall. What bothered me a lot about Edwin was his aloofness—his face always had the same blank expression. I couldn't tell if he was happy, sad, or surprised. It was as though he were dead and his eyes left open. It was his silence and detachment that discomfited me the most, and I was unnerved by his hard, relentless stare. I imagined him with a hidden gun or knife, ready to pounce over a minor request like asking him to wait to use the bathroom. I was afraid of Edwin and it didn't help matters that there were rumors of his violent tendencies.

Needless to say, it took me awhile to get used to Edwin's haunting presence. He sat in the back of the classroom, slouched in his chair, tapping the eraser end of his pencil rhythmically against the top of his desk. One of his legs was usually extended into the aisle, forcing kids to maneuver around it if they wanted to get supplies at the back of the room. Within a few days, rather than ask him to move his leg so kids could get by, I moved the materials to an area where they could avoid his outstretched limbs and taunting remarks. Planning around what wouldn't disturb Edwin became part of my routine. I placed kids near him who were strong enough to tolerate him; Edwin could make wise remarks without moving his lips, and though I never caught him throwing spitballs, I'd find them on the students or on their desks. He sat in the last seat, and the student in front of him knew not to hand him handouts or quizzes and tests. He would shove them on the floor. Or worse, he would crumble up the papers and pitch them into the trash can as though it were a basketball net. He didn't do his home-work, never raised his hand to answer or question, nor did he engage with anyone in small group discussions or activities.

I ignored Edwin as much as I could, hoping that my hands-off policy would help to keep him peaceful. I felt that I had no choice.

I knew, of course, that Edwin was not a normal eighth-grade male. That he was angry and possibly depressed was not top secret. I didn't know what he was angry about, but it was some-thing that obviously lay deep inside him and it hurt him a lot. He was Hispanic and poor, which I suppose, could account for some of the anger in this prejudiced city. Still, I thought there had to be something else.

—⊰‖⊱—

I called his mom several times and asked if she could come into the school for a conference. She refused, saying she worked long hours because Edwin's 'no good bastard of a father won't pay child support and I've got to work like a goddamned dog to support his kids. What Edwin does in school is the least of my problems'. Great. I couldn't count on the administrators to intervene either. They had already made it clear that Edwin was mine to deal with and explained that however I decided to deal with him was just fine with them.

Clearly, Edwin and I were in a lose/lose situation and the best I could do was to be respectful and kind. I knew that no one would behave like Edwin unless he was in a great deal of pain or just downright evil.

—⊰‖⊱—

Because Valentine's Day was on a Friday, the kids were more restless and unfocused than usual. Any Friday afternoon can be a challenge for teachers, particularly the last period, which can be sheer torture. I could sense an undercurrent of nervous anticipation, as though something was about to happen. Maybe there was going to be a fight between a few kids after school, or maybe some boyfriend had stopped being a boyfriend on the worst day of the year. Eighth graders take breakups *very* seriously.

Finally, the dismissal bell would ring in a matter of minutes. We had completed a good amount of work, but the room was a mess—tiny bits of paper were strewn like confetti, and highlighter caps, broken pencils, dog-eared notebooks, and textbooks were scattered as though a force of nature had barreled through and left its detritus.

My rule on days like these was to direct the kids to pick up five items and show them to me on the way out as proof that they had indeed picked up. No one could leave for the day unless he or she had contributed. The custodians appreciated my efforts; if there's anyone in a school that you want on your side, it's the custodians.

Some kids picked up a large piece of paper and tore it up into five pieces. There seemed to be a million ways to outfox me, as I soon found out. But after a while, our ritual became second nature and everyone cooperated. Except Edwin.

Edwin always strategically positioned himself to be the last one to exit—that way he couldn't pick anything up because there was nothing left. That ruse worked with my strategy to not engage unless I absolutely had to. But this day, as kids streamed by me showing their five pieces, I spotted him in the far corner of the back of the room with his hood on and his eyes downcast. He knew no hoodies were allowed. I guess he figured that with two minutes left of school there was no way I would enforce the rule.

Edwin raised his eyes just in time to catch me eyeing the hoodie. His head had been leaning against the wall and now he pulled it away to even his gaze with mine, knowing that I would be intimated and would turn away. Only I didn't. We locked gazes for only a few seconds, but those few seconds catapulted me into a reality that I had done my best for months to escape.

Edwin pulled his hoodie forward so that his eyes were barely visible. He crashed into a few of the desks and kicked books that lay on the floor as he plowed his way toward me. The kids who were left stood glued to the floor as though they, too, would be objects of his wrath if they dared move or make any noise. He shoved the girl standing in front of me to his right and she fell into the bookcase and then onto the floor. I hoped the commotion would drive the teacher on the floor below to send a student upstairs to see what was going on. Ashley, the girl who was now on the floor, looked bewildered and dazed.

He and I were face to face now. I couldn't push him aside (although it crossed my mind), because I knew that if I even brushed any part of his body, I would be accused of assault and battery. I would be the predator and not him. He stood blocking the only exit out of the classroom so I couldn't yell to one of the kids to get us some help. The help buzzer was not in my reach. I was trapped.

"I ain't picking up no trash for anybody," Edwin shouted. "And I ain't fuckin' takin' off my hoodie. Get outta my way."

The same right hand that had shoved Ashley into the bookcase now pushed me aside and I fell backward onto my desk. Thankfully, two of my students helped me get to my feet. Edwin fled down the backstairs.

"Whoa, Mrs. G., Edwin's going to be in real trouble," Nomar said.

I dreaded telling my principal, Margaret, about the incident. And now I had to worry about my car being keyed, being ambushed in the parking lot by Edwin and his friends, receiving crank calls, and things that I couldn't even imagine because even Edwin hadn't thought of them yet.

I did, of course, tell Margaret, who insisted I press charges, despite my reluctance. "You need to move forward with this," she said. "Assault and battery, at least. Ashley's parents will need to as well. Nothing ever happens to the kid because everyone is afraid to get him in trouble. I realize now that we need to start a paper trail so when he does something next time, he might be sent to the Division of Youth Services. We can't just let him do what he wants."

Like I had been doing for months.

I did end up filing charges with Juvenile Court and Edwin was sentenced to community service. Margaret suspended him from school for ten days and his mother ultimately had to come to school to readmit him.

⚔

We settled into an uneasy peace after Edwin's return from the school suspension—I tiptoed around him and he around me. I was ever watchful for signs of revenge that never surfaced. I wondered who had finally scared Edwin into some semblance of cooperation.

Edwin graduated from middle school. In the fall of his first year at the high school, Edwin assaulted a Haitian boy who was cognitively impaired. Apparently, Edwin didn't like the boy's accent nor did he like how the boy walked. The boy had sustained life-threatening injuries during the assault and it was obvious to the faculty that Edwin was out of control and needed consequences for his behavior.

The judge of the Juvenile Court recognized that Edwin needed to be punished as well. There was only one problem. Edwin was a freshman basketball star on the varsity team. He had a natural talent for the game rarely seen in a kid so young. Everyone thought that he would bring much needed glory to the high school, which had suffered through disappointing seasons for the last three years. No matter his personal failings, the high school team needed Edwin Melendez. To his credit, the judge was not swayed by the parade of character witnesses who came before him to plead for a second chance for Edwin. Some said that Edwin's actions were out of character and others claimed that his devotion to basketball would consume his free time and divert him from more aggression. The judge held firm and Edwin was sent to a juvenile corrections facility.

Many local sports fans felt that Edwin had been unfairly punished. They wrote letters to the newspaper defending his actions as those of a young restless boy who now realized the foolishness of his actions. Some writers blamed the victim for taunting Edwin, although there were no facts to support that claim.

Diehard sports fans rode around town in cars with bumper stickers that read "Free Edwin Melendez." I guess the Haitian boy's injuries didn't impress these fans as much as Edwin's athletic talent.

Edwin was freed after several years. I don't know what happened to him in the intervening years between his release and the news of his murder that was buried in the back pages of the local newspaper. The cops never found his killer.

And I never figured out why Edwin was so angry.

"GRAMPY IS PICKING ME UP"

K ate, the school adjustment counselor, and Tracy, the school social worker, worked closely together in our middle school. And when they wanted to speak to you jointly, in private, it meant that something truly horrific had happened. The two of them knew who had the deep, dark, messy secrets that everybody knows exists but no one likes to talk about. As the assistant principal, I focused on the nitty-gritty of running a school filled with middle schoolers. I worked with schedules, discipline and teams. The easy stuff.

Kate and Tracy slipped into my office and were visibly alarmed and uncomfortable as they settled around the conference table. Tracy's incisor was cutting deeply into her lower lip as she perused her notes. Kate had her eyes locked on a bumper sticker that was pinned to the bottom of my bulletin board. *Wherever you go, go with all your heart.*

"What's up?" I asked, matter-of-factly. "From the looks of you two, I'm not sure I want to hear it."

Tracy took a deep breath and turned to me. She held a pencil in her hand and methodically jabbed the table with it as she spoke. "I know that I'm going to struggle discussing this, so bear with me you guys. I've worked pretty closely with Ashley Gould and I suppose I should be glad that she trusts me enough to reveal this story, but on the other hand it adds a whole new layer to the issues we've been dealing with regarding her stepfather, her mother's passivity, her depression. We were meeting in our regular session this morning when she told me that her grandfather was molesting her. This has been going on since she was four. *Four.* That's *ten* years. She described the whole thing to me, all the sickening crap that he did for all those years. He didn't penetrate her, thank God for small favors, he just satisfied himself with that poor kid looking on. He'd sometimes have her lie down so he could spill onto her belly. Revolting."

Tracy's eyes welled up. I felt mine water as well. *So he could spill onto her* echoed in my head.

I knew that grandfather.

Every Tuesday and Thursday, Ashley went to his home after school, and I would often chat with her and the other kids who were waiting for rides. "Grampy's picking me up," she'd say when I asked if she had a ride. Sure enough, he'd show up, often twenty or thirty minutes late. He'd pull up in his colossal, red Dodge Durango truck with a cigarette dangling from the right side of his mouth. The cigarette usually had a long ash dangling from the end. The loose flesh of his cheeks lay in soft folds and the oversized glasses that he wore made his beady eyes look even smaller.

Even though he was retired, he always wore navy blue Dickie work clothes. He'd lean over to open the passenger door and say, "Hop on in, little girl!" The memory repulsed me now as I thought about how I had greeted him as though he were a loving grandfather, often making small talk—I had admired his gas-guzzling truck, his devotion to his grandchildren, the Skittles on his dashboard.

Just last week, Rick Bane, her language arts teacher, had brought down some of Ashley's writing. "The kid definitely has some talent, but the stuff she's writing about!" he exclaimed. The themes were on the dark side, mostly about adults who drank too much and children who hid under beds clutching stuffed animals. Eighth-grade girls like to write about conflicts with girlfriends and falling in like with cute boys who are oblivious to their existence, not the kind of edgy, grim material that we were seeing.

Ten years. Nobody knew. *So he could spill onto her.* I struggled to come to grips with this revelation. I ached for her. What was she thinking now that her truth was told? Was she worried about her grandfather? He would surely be angry, he would deny any allegation, and her mother would feel guilty for not discerning the truth sooner. Would Ashley, her face pimpled with adolescence and a sweet, shy smile still want to come to school? Would she think that everyone knew her secret?

Kate shattered the heavy silence. "We need to call the Department of Children and Families. There's no question of that. Where is Ashley now?"

Tracy craned her neck to see if there was a box of tissues behind her back, but seeing none, took a quick swipe at her eyes before and said, "She's sitting in the office with Patti. She's got a book that she seems to be engrossed in. I didn't want her back in class just yet. She cried a lot after she was done telling me the whole story. What a secret she had, going to that reprobate's house after school all those years knowing what was going to happen. The only thing that consoles me now is that she says he never touched her. Well, he did in his own sick way, but it wasn't the usual."

But it wasn't the usual. I wasn't sure if that made the situation better or worse. The variety of perversions that these molesters dream up always surprised me. The neighbor next door had violated me at age nine in not the "usual way" as well. Mr. B had told me to hop on his back so we could gallop around his back-yard as though he was a horse and I was his rider. My legs were wrapped around his waist and he held my knees tight against his belly. I liked Mr. B. He was so much fun compared to the rest of the parents. All they wanted to do in their spare time was wash their cars and play horseshoes. He gave us Tootsie Rolls and red lollipops shaped like sailboats. Suddenly, I felt something poking me between my legs. It felt like Mr. B's finger. I didn't know why he was poking me like that. He'd never done that before. He poked and poked but I didn't tell him to stop. I was glad when he stopped to put me down and told Arlene to hop up so she could have a turn.

"What about the police?" I asked Tracy as I tried to shake off my haunting flashback. "Shouldn't we call them?"

"DCF will get that ball rolling after they investigate. I need to call her mother. Ashley asked me not to tell her mom but I don't see how I can't. She can't go to his house after school any-more that's for sure, and I think Grampy watches her little sister on some days, too. Who knows how many kids he's violated by now."

Imagine telling your mother that her father is a heinous creature who can't be trusted with his own granddaughter. Imagine telling your mother that you know her father is a sexual pervert, that you hate him and that you *never, ever* want to see him again.

Another round of silence. I felt stuck with the horror of what we had just learned, as though we had waded too far into the ocean but didn't know how to swim. I ran my fingers through my hair as a signal that I was ready to finish up. Time for a plan. Take charge. Move this train forward.

"Ashley's mom needs to know what we know. Tracy, you seem to be the best suited to call Mrs. Gould since she has a relationship with you. Rehearse with Kate how you're going to tell her about it. You want to say it right and you want to have her emotionally stable until she can get Ashley home safely. I'll call DCF. Kate, can you bring Ashley to your office until Mom can pick her up? I think it would be best for Mrs. Gould to come after school is out so that the school is empty when she arrives. If either Ashley or mom gets emotional, they'll at least be spared an audience. Tell her to use the side door near the visitors' lot so we can be sure no one will be there but us with Ashley. Oh, and tell her to call you when she gets here, so Tracy and I can bring her to the car."

No one objected. "I'll call you to tell you how the call went," Tracy said, as she and the others left the room.

The call to DCF took only a few minutes. The screener asked perfunctory questions and I tried to answer matter-of-factly, as though I were discussing my dismay at people who eat too much fried food in my honky-tonk seaside town. She expressed no horror at what I reported. There were no exclamations of "Can you believe it?" or "I'd kill anyone who did that to my kid!" When you hear stories like this over and over again, it's difficult to lather up a frothy indignation every time abject depravity strikes.

Meanwhile, Tracy said that Mrs. Gould had seemed oddly subdued when she called. "She didn't sound surprised at *all,*" reported Tracy. "I figured she'd be incredulous, maybe question whether I had my facts straight. I was basically telling her that her father was a pervert. I thought maybe she'd try to twist the truth and make Ashley the liar. She certainly has said that Ashley exaggerates and imagines that things are worse than they are, in past conversations. From what I can gather, they don't have the best of relationships."

"Did she ask how Ashley was doing?" I asked.

"Not really. The only thing she said was 'I'll be right there,' and then she asked where Ashley was. She said to expect her in fifteen minutes or so. Ashley seems . She's got her headphones on and she's eating a cookie. The poor kid. Come on down and we can meet up with her mother together. We all need each other right now."

We all need each other right now. Tracy was right. I wanted to be alone in my office and to have a good long cry. I wanted to mourn for Ashley, for me, for all the other little girls who had to heal their way out of someone else's sickness. His creepy beady eyes nestled deep into his head. The chicken skin rustling around above his Adam's apple. His thin grey tufts of hair that poked out from under his Red Sox baseball hat. The memory of Grampy made me nauseous.

Mrs. Gould pulled up in her minivan seconds after we arrived at the visitors' entrance. Not unlike her father, she reached across the passenger's seat and opened the door for Ashley. Ashley hesitated before climbing in, stealing a glance at Tracy that portrayed her ambivalence about facing her mother. I couldn't tell if she was relieved that it was over, or if she was nervous about how her mom would react once she saw her in the flesh, bewildered and violated.

Ashley didn't speak as she reached for her seatbelt. Her mom interrupted her and reached out to pull Ashley close to her, resting her head on Ashley's thin shoulder. "Sweetheart, I am so sorry," she said emphatically. "I should have known." And then she began to cry with each new sob bearing more strength than the last. "I should have known!" she wailed. "He did it to me!"

I looked at Tracy, whose expression mirrored my incredulity and anger. What had Mrs. Gould been thinking, leaving her own child alone with her creep of a father who had done the same thing to her?

"He did the same thing to you?" Tracy asked although she knew the answer. She at least had the sense to stay calm and even. I did not.

"Yes," she said. "Obviously not the brightest idea I've ever had. And now Ashley has to suffer. I thought he had stopped. He's old. I was desperate for a sitter. Awful. I am sorry," she sobbed.

Tracy and I both stared silently at her as she cried uncontrollably. Ashley pretended to be fixated on a sparrow that was perched on the hood of the car and her gaze trailed the bird when he flew away. When Mrs. Gould finally settled down, Tracy broke the silence. "It's only natural to feel terrible in a situation like this," she started. "You're not made of stone. You'll need some good therapy,

Mrs. Gould. Get some for your whole family because this is very serious. And for tonight, just talk to each other. Take good care of Ashley. Both of you are hurting so much." Tracy couldn't offer much beyond that. "And tomorrow, I'll call to see how your evening went and we'll put together some plans for everyone to get back on track. Expect DCF to contact you soon." Tracy backed away from the car as a signal to Mrs. Gould that she could move on.

"What do you make of that news, that she, too was molested?" I whispered to Tracy. Tracy was an insightful person and I could rely on her to sort this all out, maybe help me to make some sense of all this hurt.

"So many people want their secrets to die a convenient death, as though when the secret dies, their own pain can be the coffin, all bound up, tight and buried," she explained. "We just saw where that can get you. That mother had that big secret and now not only did it hurt her, it hurt her daughter. I have a feeling this behavior has been in this family for decades. Someone must have gotten Grampy, too. Used him for sicko reasons. These things can be generational. I've seen enough of that."

I opened the door for Tracy and I slipped into the school behind her. We were silent as we made our way down the long hallway. Outside the classrooms, the teachers had hung student artwork and posters celebrating Peace Week, but we didn't have the energy to admire them. And I still had work left to do, but I knew I was spent and it wouldn't get done. I needed to be alone in my car before I got home to my kids who would be clamoring for chicken nuggets and fries.

"Tracy, 1 say, let's call it a day. Let's get on home. Get a good night's sleep. Right now, my tired soul feels like it's made of shredded wheat. I know tomorrow has to be a better day than today. It could hardly be worse."

"Amen, girl. Let's just call it the kind of day that only happens once in a lifetime. But you and I both know that that isn't the truth. But let's make it true, just for today."

HATS OFF TO LARRY!

Larry and I were in the eighth grade together. I was a special education teacher and he was a student. He was the first student I ever had with Asperger's Syndrome and I didn't know much about the condition. Not many teachers did, and although most of us had met kids a little bit like Larry through the years, we didn't know that it was something diagnosable; we just thought they were weird but *very* bright. Yes, they are socially awkward and have quirky interests, like following the patterns of water pipes in a city or memorizing bus schedules. These interests may be intense because kids with Asperger's tend to be obsessive in their thinking as well as compulsive in their actions.

Larry was a skinny teenager with a dirty blond hair, cut in a "boy's regular," the style of haircut that the barbers do for free at the Salvation Army. His skin was pale and chalky and his taupe-rimmed glasses were perched halfway up the ridge of his nose instead of parallel to his eyes. (Larry claimed to be able to see well by looking *over* his glasses instead of *through* them.) He actually was of average height and weight but he looked lanky because his clothes were too big, and I wondered if his mother deliberately bought them that way so they would last longer. His sleeves always fell one or two inches below his arms, and the seams of his pants cuffs were frayed from hanging over the backside of his sneakers. His pants were cinched so tightly at the waist that eight inches of the tongue of the belt hung down by the zipper of his pants. I suspected that Larry and his mom got their clothes from the local thrift shop.

Like most kids with Asperger's, Larry lived in a world of his own and disregarded social codes or customs. He walked down the hallways of the school dragging and rubbing his shoulder against the wall, staring up at the ceiling over his glasses. Other kids might greet him with "Hey Larry!" or even give him a friendly tap on his left shoulder, but he would shrug and stare at them. It was as if he didn't know what these advances meant, if they meant anything at all to him.

Whenever I saw Larry like this, confused and chagrined at his inability to pick up on social cues, I wanted to intervene and explain. But I knew he would be embarrassed and angry with me for observing him from afar. Larry was an eighth grader and needed to be independent, just like his peers.

I worked with Larry in small math and reading groups. The other kids ignored him most of the time, which was understandable given his compulsion to focus solely on drawing jets. He let the classroom conversations swirl around him, occasionally stopping to blink at someone who was speaking to him in an attempt to decipher the subtext. I know he found subtlety onerous and perplexing and not worth his time. There were moments when I tried to engage him in what the other kids were saying, particularly if they happened to broach a topic that I thought might interest him, but invariably Larry would rebuff me with silence or polite murmurs of dismissal. Still, I tried to spend as much time as I could with Larry because he had such strong academic abilities and his distractibility was hurting him. He was ahead of the other kids in math, and often it was Larry and I alone in another tiny room puzzling over math problems. What I didn't foresee by giving Larry so much personal attention was the jealousy of the other kids, which resulted in a bruising confrontation.

Alicia seemed to be the most resentful of the attention that Larry got from me. Her tough, demonstrative demeanor belied the fragility of her self-esteem; her harsh cry for emotional parity one morning surprised me. "Why do you pay so much attention to Larry, Mrs. G? All you do is talk about Larry, Larry, Larry, like there's no one else in the room. I think you don't like the rest of us. It's all about Larry, Larry, Larry."

"Yeah," Sarah piped in. "Why is it always all about Larry with you?"

Sarah wasn't one to speak up, but she put forth good effort this time. I hadn't realized that I had been paying so much attention to Larry. There was no excuse for my behavior, or so the two girls thought. Yet, in my mind, there certainly was a reason. Larry was a special child, quirky but lovable in his own way. I felt the need to defend myself, as well as Larry. But I couldn't do what I had to do without Larry's permission.

"Larry, do you mind if we chat about you for a minute? Can you help me explain to the girls why I give you extra help?" Larry looked up at me and nodded. The girls squirmed in their seats. I think they were surprised at my approach in dealing with their concerns.

"Girls," I began, "I know it's hard for you to see me giving Larry what you say is 'extra attention.' Larry has a condition that makes it hard for him to pay attention, and he needs a lot of help to stay focused and on task. You girls can stay focused without an adult at your side all the time, but Larry can't. Larry, do you mind if I tell them what you have?"

"No, it's OK." Larry seemed at ease so I continued.

"Larry has Asperger's. It means he has trouble learning some things, just like you do, but it also means he has trouble socializing and making friends. Larry doesn't understand the world in the same way that we do, so we all need to pitch in and help him be a success. Just like we all try to help each other succeed. We just need to help Larry a little more."

No one spoke for several seconds and the girls seemed to chew on my words without swallowing. Surprisingly, it was Larry who broke the silence.

"Yes, I have issues!" Larry pronounced with emphasis. He looked at each of them over his glasses, pushed them up to the bridge of his nose, grabbed his pencil, and then began to draw feverishly. I had never seen Larry speak directly to another student, never mind look one in the eye. His bottom teeth were raking his upper lip as the lines of his drawing grew darker. He was stressed. Had he always known he had Asperger's or was this the first time he realized that he was different? How did he feel about having issues? Was he relieved that his secret was out? Embarrassed?

Angry? Larry rarely talked about his feelings and I knew that I would probably never find out.

"Thank you Larry." I said softly. "That wasn't easy for you to say, but you had the courage to say it".

⚊╫⚊

For the rest of the school year, Larry and I worked together like two oxen pulling a five-ton load at the county fair. Larry learned ratios and proportions, and his reading skills were almost at grade level. On occasion, he tried to sneak a jet drawing into our sessions, especially if I was distracted by answering a phone or bending down to pick up a sheet of paper. I couldn't admonish Larry when his impulses to draw overtook his best intentions. If he detected any disapproval in my voice, he grew silent and looked down at his desk. Nothing I said would dissuade him from giving me the silent treatment, which sometimes lasted for an hour or so. After a few bouts of a brooding Larry shutting me out, I figured out that the best course was to stay completely focused on Larry so that he would then stay focused with me.

And so, his grades began to improve and he made the honor roll for the next three quarters. I was thrilled when he was identified as provisionally qualified for the National Junior Honor Society, but he faced two more hurdles before being inducted. He needed to perform fourteen hours of community service and to prove that he had "leadership" qualities. I knew that community service was going to be hard for Larry, so I approached the coordinator of the program and proposed that Larry engage in service of any kind, which could include service at home. She approved and his mom agreed to supervise him. Larry folded socks, swept the kitchen floor, and wiped down countertops for his service. She was prouder of Larry than he was of himself. "I know Larry has a good brain and will make something of himself!" she exclaimed to me on the phone when I called for a progress update. "I've always said, 'Don't underestimate my Larry!' His father may be a bum but he won't be!'"

Meanwhile, I was stymied as to how I could help Larry be a leader. With his head hung low as he ambled down the hallway, his self-effacing body language, and his inability to make eye contact, he wasn't exactly the type of person that inspired your average eighth grader. He could be funny on occasion, but being funny once in a while doesn't make you a leader. It bothered me that Larry had made some good academic and social progress, but in the end he would be rejected from the honor society because he wasn't a leader. Life sure wasn't fair for kids like Larry.

The honor society candidates had to provide their own proof of leadership by writing an essay about their personal experiences as a leader. The essays were intended to help the candidates reflect on their character and how they became role models for other kids. The students had to write these essays independently, and as I watched Larry compose on his own, I worried about his reaction if he were to be rejected from membership because of something that wasn't his fault. In my mind, he was so vulnerable, with his barely audible voice and slow, hesitant manner. I had to brace for the inevitable, and worked and reworked how I would phrase what I had to say in the most positive way I could imagine. I would have to let Larry down easy.

The best three essays were going to be announced at the first practice session for the induction ceremony. As a reward, the winners were going to read their essays at the ceremony. The co-ordinator and the teachers began to make plans for the rehearsals and I heard no murmurings about students being excluded at the last minute. I didn't dare ask about Larry, fearing that I might trigger an upsetting response.

Larry showed up at the first rehearsal dressed in khaki pants, a light blue long sleeved shirt and a navy blue vest. He didn't seem to notice that the other kids were dressed in their usual grunge wear. Larry's mom had certainly done a good job getting him outfitted.

The coordinator spent some time getting the kids situated on the stage. The boys were seated in the back and the girls in the front, their knees pulled together and their feet flat on the floor. The coordinator then reviewed the procedures that she expected them to follow.

I looked at Larry up on the stage. His face was expressionless and I could see his knee vibrating up and down, up and down with a steady beat. I knew that the commotion was getting on his nerves. I wanted to scramble up the side stairs and slip him a piece of paper and a pencil to draw his streamlined jets. That would have calmed Larry for sure.

"I need your attention," the coordinator began. "The speakers that I name will come up to the podium, and I will give them their speeches to read. I'll show you how to adjust the microphone when you come up." She paused now to make sure that the crowd was completely silent before announcing the name of the first speaker that had been chosen to speak. Drumroll please... "And the first National Junior Honor Society speaker for 2005 is Larry Anderson!"

The auditorium was completely quiet as the crowd absorbed what no one had anticipated. Then someone yelled, "Go Larry!" and the inductees clapped enthusiastically.

Smiling sheepishly, Larry made his way to the podium. The coordinator helped him with the microphone. When he began to read, his voice was barely audible and he didn't make eye contact with the audience at any point. His reading was slow and dysfluent. He stuttered several times. The coordinator crept up to his side and whispered, "Larry, no one can hear you. Can you speak a little louder for us?"

Larry straightened his back and glanced over at me. I mouthed, "Louder Larry, go for it!" He smiled a half-smile, and picked up his essay so that it was no longer sitting flat on the desk part of the podium.

"I showed leadership once," Larry began. "I was in the seventh grade and I was on the bus sitting next to a friend of mine who also has issues. A sixth grader came up to where we were sitting and he wanted me to move so he could have my seat. I knew that boy was up to no good because I had seen him pick on my friend before and I didn't like it one bit. He wanted to bother my friend by punching him in the arm and trying to get him to cry so other kids would laugh at him. I stood right up to him and told him, 'We don't like bullies in this school. I don't like bullies and I won't let you pick on my friend. Go back to your own seat and leave us alone.' I was scared when I did that but I'm glad I did. No one should have to put up with bullies. I say, 'Why can't we all just be happy like the Chinese?' Thank you."

It was hard to figure out how the bully responded by the way that Larry told the story. But I knew that when Larry had decided to take the bullying matter into his own hands, he had harnessed a power in himself that he didn't know he had. Picturing Larry on the bus, forcing a bully to back down, as I hoped the bully had, made my eyes water and I glanced at the other teachers, who also wiped away tears.

Larry looked at me to indicate that he was done and then turned to walk back to his seat. And the kids, "Larry, Larry, Larry...."

I LIKE MY CATS

Donna Gillis and I had taught for four years in the same middle school but had never met.

However, I did know a lot about her, thanks to teachers' room gossip. She was an eighth-grade language arts teacher with a mailbox, an email address, and a phone extension number. Still, few ever communicated with her because she was rarely in the building. Donna was always out sick.

The gossip turned ferocious as soon as we got back after the summer vacation. And with good reason. Donna had raided the sick bank once again.

In many school systems, union contracts allow teachers to voluntarily donate sick days to a sick bank. The sick bank helps teachers who run out of their allotted days due to long term illnesses. Instead of being forced off the payroll, they can continue to collect a salary by using the sick time assigned to their coworkers. It's like stowing away money for a rainy day.

Of course, we all donated to the bank regularly. We were like foxhole buddies in this urban jungle and we happily helped and supported each other. But this time, when we got the memo telling us that the balance was low, the resentment was palpable.

Donna's work patterns were a study in calculated efficiency. She knew how to manipulate her union rights just as well as some corporate tax attorneys know how to cheat the IRS.

Donna was a master of her craft. Show up for work. Get sick with anything that exacerbates asthma like a cold, flu, or pneumonia. Shop around for a doctor who will attest to how perilous it is to be around a lot of kids who harbor germs and other health hazards. Stay out of work until the last possible moment when you will lose your job unless you return for a certain amount of days.

In October, I finally met Donna on a field trip. The eighth-grade teachers were taking three hundred kids on a field trip and we were chaperones on the same bus.

I took attendance, reviewed good bus behavior rules, and chastised the kids that had three in a seat rather than two. I craned my neck to check the back seats, often getting up and strolling the aisle to make sure the kids were behaving. While I managed this controlled chaos, Donna read *People* magazine.

It was also obvious to me that the energy Donna had poured into getting sick days was not matched by an interest in her appearance. Her hair was streaked with grey and hung down her back in a long single braid. She wore no makeup which exposed old acne scars from her teenage years forty years ago. Her blue cardigan sweater was way too small. A man's Timex watch on her wrist was her only jewelry. What looked like clumps of white animal fur clung to her grey woolen slacks.

When Donna had finished reading her magazine, she stared out the window. I interrupted her. "This is quite a welcome back," I said. "Your first day and you're on a field trip with a mob of kids, inhaling gas fumes and other sweet delights." I chuckled, hoping she would see the humor of being in a decrepit old bus filled with thirteen-year-olds.

"Oh yeah," she said. "My doctor tells me to avoid closed spaces with lots of people because of my asthma and here I am. It isn't like the powers that be actually listen to anything that I have to say about my health, or heaven forbid, that they would even care. I should be back at the school working with the six kids that had to be left behind."

"You have asthma?" I said. "How bad is it?" I knew she had asthma but didn't know the severity.

"Bad. I have a lot of attacks and I can't go anywhere. I mean I won't go anywhere without my inhalers. I'm on a nebulizer four times a day. I'm allergic to everything. It's not an easy way to live." Donna stared out the window again.

I knew she was trying to avoid me, but I wasn't willing to let go just yet.

"If you're as sick as you say and shouldn't be around kids, why don't you retire? You've been teaching a while haven't you?"

"Yes, yes I have. Twenty-eight years to be exact. If I retire now, I'd go out at sixty-eight percent of my salary, not enough to retire.

I need three more years so I can get eighty percent. I have no husband, no parents, no children. I'm totally, totally alone in the world except for my cats and my cigarettes. They're what keep me going."

"Is it your cats that you're allergic to?" I asked.

Donna nodded. "But I'm not getting rid of my babies. I don't care what my doctor says or how much trouble I have breathing. I'm not getting rid of my babies. They're my family." The bus driver looked in his rear view mirror when he heard her voice rise.

"I'm sure your doctor's not crazy about your smoking," I mused. "You must be a light smoker."

"Ha! Are you kidding me? When I smoke one pack a day, it's a damn good day.

Every time I visit a doctor I tell him, 'Look, I smoke. Get it? I'm not going to quit until I'm good and ready and right now I'm not good and I'm not ready. If you're going to badger me, tell me now so I won't waste my time and money nor will I waste yours.' I've had this same conversation with three or four different doctors. Now I've got a doctor who's smart enough to keep his mouth shut and just write up the doctor's notes so I can keep coming in, getting sick, staying home and coming back. For the next three years."

I couldn't think of anything to say. Donna disgusted me. Having actually articulated her plan of draining the sick bank regularly was pretty dumb on her part, never mind unethical. What a thief.

⭬⭯

The next time Donna cycled through one of her sick routines, Margaret, the school principal, didn't allow her back in the classroom. Margaret was a no nonsense administrator whom I often thought to be unforgiving and ruthless. However, I did admire her when she took a stand and did what was right for kids. Someone without Margaret's strength of character might have backed down and continued to play games for the sake of keeping peace with the union.

It wasn't fair to the kids either. They needed consistency in the classroom, not an absent teacher half the year. The problem was that Donna needed to have something to do, some sort of job in the school. Margaret had a brilliant idea.

The seventh-grade urinals had been overflowing on a regular basis because boys were stuffing toilet paper in the drain. Margaret decided to put Donna in charge of handing out paper towels, manning a sign-in sheet and keeping track of who went in and out of the bathroom. With Donna as a sentry parked outside the boys' room, the problem with the urinals and cleanup complaints would be solved.

I had mixed feelings the first day I spotted Donna, ensconced in her folding chair at the entrance of the boys' restroom. She had her ubiquitous magazine in her lap. I knew that a classroom was no place for this woman, but her new role was humiliating and a violation of union rules. Margaret had few options for driving Donna out of the profession, and subterfuge seemed to be the only answer after all these years. I secretly cheered for Margaret even though I knew that I was shirking my obligations to Donna as the building's union rep.

I worked my way back to my classroom and snuck another peek at Donna. Several boys went into the restroom and then came out.

Donna had not even lifted her head in acknowledgment. She was doing about as good a job with her new duties as she did teaching.

After a few days of bathroom duty, Donna decided to complain. She sought me out, expecting a sympathetic ear because of my union position. "I'm a certified teacher for crying out loud and Margaret put me in the bathroom. That's insulting! I thought it was just for a few days, but now I find out that it's my permanent position. She says that I've ruined enough lives during the last few years. I can't help that. Isn't that bathroom gig a violation of my rights? She can't do this, can she?"

She was right about the rules violation. But Margaret was right about Donna being a poor excuse for a teacher. She didn't deserve our sick bank days, her union benefits, and her taxpayer-paid salary. She was an embarrassment to all of us and I wanted her out. For once, Margaret and I were on the same team.

"She is doing it," I said. "Who's going to stop her? Not me. My advice? And forgive me for being so blunt but it's time to fold your tent and go home to your cats. Really."

I had been seething mad for weeks. Aside from robbing the taxpayers, she was robbing kids of an education, and she was robbing dignity from our profession. I wanted to say a lot more but I didn't because it would serve no purpose.

"Really? Don't you understand that I'm sick? I don't understand why everyone is picking on me." She was visibly upset.

"They're picking on you because you're a crook," I said. "You're malingering and pretending that you're a teacher so you can retire with enough money to pay your bills. You don't give a shit about anybody in this school and frankly, we're all sick of it."

Donna folded her arms and gave me a hardened stare. "Some building rep you are. What a phony. Pretending that you're a champion of fairness and equity."

Donna's cutting retort stung. She had a point. I was supposed to defend her right to a position on par to the one to which she was hired. Anyone could see that I was remiss in my duties.

"I don't pretend. I am. Being fair is encouraging you to do what's right. And if you have an ounce of morality left in you, you'll retire. Soon."

I stormed down the hall, still wondering if I had done the right thing by not going to bat for Donna. But then I considered that not one teacher had come to me to ask about Donna's assignment. Their silence told me they gave consent. I thought about apologizing, but I wasn't sorry. I resigned myself to the fact that there was no good solution. I avoided Donna as best I could. I was angry, embarrassed and slightly remorseful.

⚒

After a week had passed, Martha announced to the teachers in the faculty room that she had heard that Donna was submitting her papers to retire.

I was relieved, of course. The only downside to Donna's retirement at sixty-eight percent of her salary was that it was fifty percent more than she deserved.

"I WANT JENNA TO HAVE FUN!"

M r. Pino arrived early for his daughter's annual special education meeting on the last Wednesday in May. Jenna was
an eighth grader who was entering high school in the fall, and the
agenda called for a review of the last year's progress and the plan
for next year. As her special education teacher, I was responsible
for chairing the meeting.

Jenna's parents were never married and lived separately. Jenna
talked about her father often, but I had never met him. He did not
have custody but he seemed to be the coordinator of Jenna's weekend plans, including time when she and her cousins had sleepovers
at his apartment that sat atop a marine supply store.

On any given Wednesday, at the end of the school day, Jenna
would typically announce that she and her cousins were going to
McDonald's 'with my daddy'. Sometimes she would describe other
plans that he had for them following their fast- food outing, like
bowling, movies, or skeeball at the local amusement park. The trips

would typically end at her father's apartment where they would watch videos and devour Coke, chips and Snicker bars.

It was clear that Mr. Pino was a Disneyland daddy, the kind of guy who has a lot of fun with the kids but deals with none of the drudge. Translation: Jenna never did homework on Wednesday nights.

While waiting for Mr. Pino to enter the meeting room, I reflected on Jenna. Her school year had been a disaster. She barely passed because she was so distractible. I often caught her staring into space, twirling a strand of her long brown hair between her finger and her thumb. If I called her name to get her attention, she continued to stare, oblivious to everything but her own quiet thoughts.

Some days after the dismissal bell had rung, she'd poke her head through the doorway and ask for extra math help. Even though I knew we wouldn't be getting much math work done, I'd welcome her, of course, putting away whatever I'd been working on. Asking for math help was Jenna's way of saying she wanted to talk about friends and Daddy.

The door swung open and Mr. Pino entered. He was a man who looked to be in his mid-sixties and I was surprised to see how old he was. He must have been close to fifty when Jenna was born. He was of average weight and build, and despite his balding pate, surprisingly handsome and fit. He was neatly dressed in black pants and a red polo shirt. I invited him to have a seat.

While we waited for the other people to arrive, he'd glance often at his watch. He alternated checking his watch with running his fingers through the few wisps of hair that remained. I decided to engage him in conversation, hoping to distract him from his obsessive checking and stroking. "Jenna tells me you just retired. That must be fun. You can hang around with your friends as much as you'd like." Ugh. I didn't know why I said this.

Mr. Pino checked his Timex before responding.

"Oh, I don't know about that," he said. "I really don't have any friends. All they want is your money and to get in your personal business. I actually avoid friends. I used to be pretty popular at the high school in my younger day. Do you believe that I was the captain of the football team and the baseball team? Look it up if you don't believe me. I was a great athlete when I was young. I played in the district finals, too. Made the baseball All-Star team. I was always in the papers."

Given his muscular build and the self-assured way he carried himself, I didn't have any reason not to believe him. But why didn't a local guy with a storied past in a working class town have any friends?

"Well, how do you stay busy in retirement?" I asked. I knew that this was none of my business, but my curiosity got the best of me.

"Oh, I'm busy watching my videos, playing on the computer, and taking Jenna and my nieces out like I will today. Those kids are something else. I also drive her mother around because she doesn't have a car. She's too dumb to drive and she lives right around the corner so it's not a problem. The guy in the marine shop has me deliver parts around town a few times per week so I'm pretty busy."

I didn't like that he was calling Jenna's mother dumb but I didn't correct him. Considering our tenuous relationship, challenging him at this point would have been like yanking a dog's tail while scratching behind his ears. It was obvious that he had an inflated opinion of himself, probably stemming from his glory days as a winsome jock.

The other team members and Jenna's mother, Winnie, trickled into the meeting. After the introductions and the progress review, it was time to put together a schedule of classes for freshman year in high school. To save time, I had put together a proposed schedule and hoped that the team and Jenna's parents would approve.

"Let me show you what I think next year's schedule should look like," I said, passing around copies of the schedule. "As you can see, she'll be in four special ed classes which will have very small numbers so she'll get lots of attention, one general ed class, and two electives. I think it's an ideal schedule for Jenna and if she has this type of course load every year, she'll graduate right on time."

"I like it," Winnie said with no trace of hesitation. She had said very little in the meeting, but had listened intently.

"What do *you* know?" Mr. Pino asked Winnie who was seated beside him. "*You* never *went* to high school!"

"I'm just saying it sounds good for Jenna. Small classes, lots of attention."

Winnie looked at Mr. Pino for affirmation which appeared to be a habit of hers— offer an opinion and check with the boss to make sure it's the correct opinion to have. Mr. Pino averted her gaze and stared at me with steely eyes.

"This schedule is way too demanding," he said. "High school is supposed to be fun. She won't be having any fun going to all these classes."

Beads of sweat formed in one of the cracks of his forehead. He raked his skull several times. I stared at him dumbfounded.

"Actually, this is the lightest schedule I can put together and still have Jenna graduate on time," I explained. "And Mr. Pino, high school should be about learning and growing, not just about fun. I mean, we all want the kids to have fun, but that shouldn't be the main goal. Jenna needs to graduate from high school so she can have a good life, get a decent job."

"She'll have a good life as long as I'm around. She can't count on her dimwit mother here, working half the time at the motel, half the time being on welfare. I don't want Jenna spending her time doing homework, worrying about writing papers. She's half-retarded like her mother here. Can't you see that or do I have to educate you? We don't need to waste her time. I want Jenna to have fun."

I needed to disarm him before he insulted Winnie more. How do you reason with someone who wants his daughter to go to high school solely for the fun?

"Mr. Pino, I'm sorry to disappoint you, but this is the best I can do for Jenna right now. To offer her less would be a tremendous disservice and I know this team will agree that this schedule of classes meets her needs and capabilities."

Mr. Pino paused to take a deep breath and then fixed his icy gaze at me. "That's what I hate about all government workers. Wanting to know all about my personal life that is none of their business. Telling people what they should do, when they should do it, how they do it. I don't understand why I can't do what I want for my own child here, my precious daughter who means the world to me. I can't trust the mother here to do what's right. She doesn't even know what you're talking about. She can't even read. Bet you didn't know that."

Winnie looked my way, her eyes beginning to water with the humiliation of her secret now revealed. Her shoulders were slumped forward and she looked down at her lap. I wanted to put my arms around her. And I wanted to slap Mr. Pino for hurting Winnie with his hateful, caustic words.

"You listen here!" I was angry and my voice shook. "You don't have to like what we do here, but you *do* have to follow the law. This schedule is the lightest that I can arrange, and Winnie is her legal guardian who has to approve it. We can take your opinion under advisement but the signature that we have to honor is Winnie's. And please, I welcome your input on Jenna's education, but your opinions about team members sitting in this meeting are not welcome, and personally, I find your remarks very offensive."

"You don't have to go gettin' all huffy about it," he said. "I want my daughter to have fun. Is that so bad? You can't seem to see the logic of this so I obviously can't help you and you apparently can't help me." He stood up so abruptly that his chair toppled. He stuffed his papers into a manila folder and headed toward the door. "And don't bother ever invitin' me to one of these again cuz I ain't comin'.

No one spoke and the silence seemed to suck the air out of the room. Even though I knew I was right and I had won the battle, I felt defeated. He had left raging mad and I wondered if Winnie and Jenna would suffer as a result. He didn't strike me as the forgetful type, especially after being denied his wishes. Winnie had completely broken down by now, sobbing softly. There was nothing left to do but apologize to the group for this sad turn of events and to adjourn the meeting.

⇐⊹⊹⇒

Fast forward to one evening at the start of summer vacation. While seated at my kitchen table, a headline in the local newspaper caught my eye. It read, "Local man arrested on multiple counts of child rape out on bail." The article was about Mr. Pino, who had been arrested and charged with multiple counts of child rape and aggravated assault. Although the minors were unnamed, I knew they were Jenna and her cousins.

The article described the condition of Mr. Pino's apartment as filthy beyond belief with piles of pornographic videos and magazines stacked in every corner. An investigation into the hard drive of Mr. Pino's computer revealed a long history of visits to a variety of child pornographic sites, which according to the police, the girls had viewed on many occasions.

My stomach somersaulted. I was disgusted by the description of the apartment and the pervasiveness of the pornographic magazines, videos and sex toys. I imagined the girls playing along at first, maybe thinking it was fun or even funny, and then realizing that they had been bribed with fast food, candy and CDs. I pictured the monstrous Mr. Pino verbally haranguing the girls if they resisted his advances, threatening them with reprisals if the secret was leaked to any adults.

The arrest of Mr. Pino explained Jenna's daydreaming, the disengagement, the visits to talk after school, the furtive giggling about male sexual parts. Now she had to deal with the shame of having been involved in these sordid activities and guilt for daddy getting caught.

Mr. Pino insisted that he could advocate for himself at his arraignment and told the judge that he was not guilty of any crimes because "the age of consent for sexual activity which is sixteen in our state is way too high and should be adjusted to age twelve."

I was right about the delusions of grandeur and his narcissism. What I should have figured out was that a man with no friends, who is concerned about government workers prying into his personal business, and who insists that his daughter have plenty of time for fun as a high school student is probably what I should have known was "a person of interest". Of the worst kind.

IF YOU DON'T TELL, NEITHER WILL I

Mateo was the middle school clotheshorse. His problem was that the school committee had decided that uniforms were mandatory.

I often spotted Mateo in the schoolyard, preening and thoroughly enjoying the love and admiration of his fellow seventh graders.

One day, Mateo arrived sporting a pair of expensive jeans, no doubt hoping that no one would notice the difference between the dark indigo of his jeans and the navy blue dress code pants. While I waited for him at the top of the stairs, I saw Joan, the principal, parked in her usual spot just inside the entrance. She wasted no time when it came to letting kids know when there were dress code violations.

"Mateo," she reprimanded, "you best be hauling your sorry self to my office with those fancy schmancy jeans you got on. You're not fooling anyone, least of all me."

Mateo walked up the steps and didn't bother to turn around to acknowledge Joan.

"Did you hear me young man?"

"OK, OK, I'll be there. Calm down!"

"You better be, tough guy."

⋯ ⊷⊶ ⋯

When Mateo didn't arrive in class after an hour or so, I assumed he'd been assigned to in-house suspension, given that this was his fifth offense. I had a planning period, so I made my way to the former chapel in the convent across the way so I could do my work without being interrupted.

The chapel still had the old altar in place, a rectangular solid stone table that I used for my desk. I had to be careful when I crossed the stained carpet because the wrinkles in it were like undulating waves and I had tripped several times. I was so focused on not falling that I didn't even notice Mateo, folded in the corner, his head leaning into his knees.

⋯ ⊷⊶ ⋯

After my allotted forty-five minutes, I stood to leave. As I put on my coat, I spotted him.

"Mateo, what in the world are you doing here?"

Silence.

"Mateo, why are you here?"

"I don't want to go to class! Not in these pants!"

"What pants?" I didn't see any unusual pants."

"These sweatpants, they have holes in them, they're embarrassing. I don't wear big old baggy sweatpants like poor kids do."

From what I knew, Mateo *was* poor. His parents both worked the night shift at a plastic factory, which didn't exactly generate a formidable income. I wondered how his parents could afford the expensive clothes he wore. It's one thing to be poor, but quite another to look poor.

"Mrs. Rappaport said that I can't wear my jeans because of the dress code so I have to wear these. I ain't going back to class with these pants. No way. I don't dress at no Goodwill. Can I stay here? Please?" He eyes welled with tears.

"Please, Mrs. G! Please, I can't let my friends see me like this."

The adult in me wanted to tell him he better scram to the classroom before we both get in trouble. But then a sixth-grade flashback took over.

I was seated in the front row of Sr. Madeleine Paul's class. She was statuesque and square-jawed with horn-rimmed glasses that belong on a banker's face. I felt something warm in my underwear.

It had happened enough times so that I recognized what it was. It was that time of month and I needed to take care of what I knew would be a big mess very soon.

I raised my hand. I was sure everyone was looking at me.

"Mona, yes?" Sister was the type that wasted no time.

"Sister, may I please go to the girl's room? I would like to go right now."

"You know the rule. It's 1:30. Didn't you go after lunch? An hour ago?"

"Yes, I did. But I need to go again. Please!"

"You can wait till three o'clock. When school gets out. You're a big girl. I know you can wait."

Just because I was big didn't mean I didn't need to use a bathroom. There was no use. I knew that. I couldn't very well tell her my reason for wanting the bathroom. I would have to sit there and wait.

I couldn't concentrate on whatever it was Sister was teaching that day. I felt the blood spreading into the back of my uniform jumper. By the time the bell rang, I knew my backside was soaked. Boys would laugh. They would know I had my period. They would make me miserable.

I waited for most of my fifty-two classmates to file out before I finally got up. I looked down, and saw a large bloodstain on my wooden seat. I clasped my hands behind my back and tried to cover my backside as best I could while I made my way to my coat, which hung on a hook outside the classroom. Some boy was certainly going to spot that stain and point it out to all his friends. That stain had to be removed fast—everyone knew it was my seat.

I ran to the basement to the girls' bathroom and gathered some toilet paper, balled it up and then wet it. I rushed upstairs to clean my seat, hoping Sister was still on yard duty, scattering the kids so they would make their way home to mothers with aprons and pot roasts in the oven. Mothers who were never told when the nuns did wrong.

Thankfully, when I returned, I was alone in the classroom to clean up the remnants of my shame. As soon as I was done cleaning, I scooted out the door as fast as I could and ran home.

Mateo still sat in the corner, his chin perched on his knees. Tears flowed freely down his cheeks and he made no move to hide them.

"Please Mrs. G., let me stay here till after school. I can't let the kids to see me in these sweatpants. I can't."

I could still feel the sixth-grade anxiety I had experienced that afternoon, the fear of being caught with blood on the seat and of roaming the hall with a bull's eye on my backside. The poor kid was staring at me now, waiting for me to make up my mind.

"Sit in that corner over there and I don't want to hear a peep out of you. Don't leave when the bell rings. Wait for me to come over here and get you. I'll take you to the door and you can head on home. Get your books out and do your work. Do something useful."

Mateo folded his lips so that they were now invisible. He looked like a chicken headed for slaughter that couldn't believe it was being spared and kept as a pet. It was one of the few times in my teaching career that I knew I had a friend for life. And maybe in a whole lot of trouble if I got caught.

I was relieved that he would be free of torment and ridicule. But I had to make sure that no one knew that I had left him in the building unattended or I would be fired for sure.

"And one last thing Matty, if you don't tell, neither will I."

IT DOESN'T GET ANY BETTER THAN THAT

The middle school television studio was packed with kids. The final round of the Geography Bee was being broadcast throughout the school, and even though I was just an onlooker, I was giddy with anticipation.

Ten seventh graders were facing off with ten eighth graders. These kids were the best of the bunch and had already defeated more than five hundred classmates in many rounds.

By the second hour of the show, eighteen kids had been eliminated in the fast-paced competition. Eighth-grader Andrew Papandrea and seventh grader Ryan Bravura remained the last men standing. They were seated next to each other facing Mr. Pike, the social studies teacher and moderator.

Ryan was known far and wide for his command of obscure geographical facts. He was obsessed with geography, but the word on the street was that Andrew was favored to keep his title. He had won last year as a lowly seventh grader but now he appeared much older. He was broad-shouldered, had a budding mustache and his hands were like bear claws. He wore a striped tie.

Baby-faced Ryan barely weighed ninety pounds and his hair was a tangled mess of black curls. He had delicate features and was perfectly cast as an elf in last year's Christmas play.

The special education teacher in me naturally roots for the underdog and I prayed to Saint Jude for Ryan to clinch the win. Of course, I outwardly had to appear unbiased.

Ryan had Asperger's Syndrome. Sometimes the obsessions that characterize this syndrome were an asset, like when it was time to focus on geography, but sometimes they could get in Ryan's way. For kids with Asperger's, life can be very challenging especially during the teenage years.

Several weeks ago, I was called into Ms. Nolan's class because Ryan was agitated and having difficulty calming down. He was upset about the tune that was played over the intercom prior to the principal's daily announcements. Ryan had expected the same tune that is played every day and didn't understand why there was a change. I tried to reason with him, telling him that the CD must be lost or broken and that the change was actually a welcome one.

"Aren't you getting tired of hearing the same old thing day after day?" I asked.

He insisted that the change was making him very uncomfortable and only agreed to settle down after I promised to replace the CD by the next morning.

The following week the French teacher, Ms. Dubois, sought my advice when Ryan became the victim of unrequited love. He stared relentlessly at one of her students, Cheyenne, a petite, blond seventh-grade girl who complained that he was stalking her on Facebook and sneaking up on her at her locker. "All I know is that he makes me feel creepy and I don't know how to handle it," she explained. "I know he means no harm and he's really, really sweet, but can you get him to stop?"

Ms. Dubois and I arranged to have a meeting with him after school. We said that we understood that he had deep feelings for Cheyenne, but that he made her uncomfortable. We tried to be gentle and kind but he broke down and cried uncontrollably. His mother called the next day to report that Ryan was horribly depressed and wouldn't be returning to school for a few days.

So here we were. Clearly, after the events of the last few weeks, Ryan needed a win. Cheyenne was right—he was a little weird but really sweet.

Andrew's demeanor was impressive as he sat poised for Mr. Pike's questions, which increased in difficulty. His responses were crisp and immediate, and he maintained his composure even though the pressure was building.

"This is for Andrew: 'Which country's capital is located on an island in West Africa?'" Mr. Pike asked.

For the first time, Andrew did not seem confident. He looked down at the floor. I could tell that he hadn't the foggiest.

"Ghana?" Andrew asked, hopeful but unconvinced.

"No, it's Equatorial Guinea. Sorry, Andrew. Ryan has to answer the next question correctly before you are eliminated."

"Now for the next question. Ready Ryan?"

Ryan chewed his lips in anticipation and his right knee jittered, bouncing up and down. His eyes were focused on Mr. Pike.

The students shifted in their seats. The kids weren't supposed to make any noise but a few yelled out, "Go Ryan!" Others shushed them. Mr. Pike posed the next question: "What is the term for the fan-shaped feature composed of sand and gravel that is formed where a stream emerges from a mountain valley onto a plain?"

Ryan put his palm to his forehead. "I know it, I know it! " he said enthusiastically. "Alluvial fan." He looked at Mr. Pike who paused for a long few seconds before announcing, "*You* are right! Ryan Bravura is the winner of the Geography Bee."

The seventh graders jumped out of their seats and rushed to Ryan, crowding him like the Red Sox in a World Series win.

I loved this. Like Andrew last year, Ryan became an overnight middle school celebrity. Not only was he really, really, sweet. He was really, really, smart.

MY DAD IS MY HERO

I couldn't allow Ryan Connors to get on the bus after school, not after throwing a tantrum an hour before the dismissal buzzer. In all my years of teaching, and as assistant principal in this middle school, I had never seen an emotional breakdown like this one.

Ryan slapped Matthew so hard that his handprint was still on Matthew's face five minutes later. Telling Ryan minutes before dismissal that he was going to be suspended was good thinking: I didn't want the rest of the teachers and students to be subjected to his antics after he heard the news. He might run through the hallways screaming, barge into classrooms or bulldoze his way into the nurse's office to accuse her of lying about the extent of Matthew's injury.

Sure enough, Ryan kicked the chairs around my conference table, tore announcements off my bulletin board and screamed obscenities. This kid wasn't used to being punished when he misbehaved. Ryan insisted he was completely innocent. He even wrote a statement describing his version of the events, "I would say I touched a kid's cheek because he said I stink, but I didn't even hurt him. I had witnesses say it wasn't hard, and the kid still turns around and tells. And now I get suspended for no reason."

As part of his statement, he was asked to name an adult who was a positive influence in his life and what that person would think of his behavior. He wrote: "An adult that has been a positive influence on my life is my dad. He is my hero because he fought in Iraq. Also, he is trying to be the best father he can be. He is my best friend. He's more of a friend than my dad and I like that."

⊷⊶

I didn't know what response I would get when I called the Connors' home. It was the beginning of the school year and hadn't yet met his parents, but I couldn't imagine what kind of people could raise such an angry, undisciplined child as Ryan. To my surprise, Mrs. Connors was quite receptive and arrived within ten minutes of my call to take Ryan home. Ryan had calmed down, but he still was upset. Mrs. Connors asked if Ryan could sit outside my office so she could speak to me in private. I agreed that was a good idea.

"I'd like to tell you about things that are going on at home so you can understand why Ryan acts the way he does," she began. "And please call me Lisa—I'm only thirty-one."

I immediately warmed to Lisa. She had a mane of curly black hair that covered most of her shoulders and she had high cheekbones, a nod to her Native American ancestry. Her hot pink sweater fit snugly over her leggings.

113

"Let's sit here at the table," I suggested. "I hope I didn't take you away from something important. I know how precious time without kids is when you need to get stuff done."

"The bus that Katy, my daughter, takes won't get to my house till four o'clock so we have plenty of time," she said. "Should I begin?"

I nodded.

"I don't know if you know this but my husband, Drew, just got home from Iraq. He's been there three times, three times! He left me with Ryan and Katy, who needs twenty-four-hour care because of a birth injury that left her totally incapacitated."

"You've certainly got your hands full," I said.

"Oh yeah. So, when my husband left for Iraq, I told him, 'Drew, when you get over there do what you have to do.' I meant in the women department. When those guys go over there, who knows if they're coming back or in what shape they'll be in if they make it back. God forbid. He has a friend who came back with no chin. He can't eat, he can't drink, he can't talk. 'Live it up,' I told him. 'Just don't tell me about it.' He's in the Reserves so don't you know he goes over there and falls in love with a woman in his unit and she lives nearby, practically in our backyard."

"So, now he still loves that woman? Is that the problem?"

"Well, no. He broke up with her when he got back and she was madder than a hatter when he did that. She's not married with kids so she doesn't get it. Ryan came home after school a few weeks ago, and he goes to check the messages on the phone like he usually does, sometimes he's looking to see if you called by the way, and she left a message describing what she and my husband did in bed in Iraq."

The conversation had grown uncomfortable. "Lisa, you and your husband are still together?"

"Well, sort of. He moved out two weeks ago, but not with her. He moved because of the neighbors across the street. You see, while my husband was gone, I fell in love with Joe Azadikian. I think you must know his kids, Adrianna and Tyler? Twins in seventh grade? Well, the Azadikians were our best friends before Drew left for Iraq, and after he left they helped me a lot, especially with Katy. His wife doesn't know about this, of course. The only people who know are me, my husband, Joe, and now you. I told Drew that I never had sex with Joe, it was all computer sex, but he said it doesn't matter, that I ruined the marriage. Honestly, I'd rather be with Joe than Drew. Drew is too bossy."

"Well, this is all very interesting," I said, "but let me tell you about what happened to Ryan today because I have another parent arriving shortly."

Although Lisa assured me that she and her husband would discourage Ryan's attacks, he got into more fights as the months wore on. In fact, Ryan became too dangerous for us to allow him to be around the other kids. His team of teachers felt that Ryan would benefit from placement in an alternative program. While the school psychologist and I waited for Ryan to be escorted to my office for a meeting to discuss his new placement, Drew Connors arrived. I was pleased I was finally going to meet Drew, and even more thankful that he had agreed to come to the meeting in the event Ryan needed to be subdued.

Drew was an extremely attractive, tall man with salt and pepper hair and groomed, matching beard. It was easy to see how that female reservist had fallen in love with him.

"What are you thinking?" I asked Drew after we had all introduced ourselves.

Drew pensively rubbed his chin and said, "What am I thinking? Well, I'm thinking how sad I am that it's come to this. That I'm probably at fault for Ryan's acting out. I love him, and I hope that he knows that. He also knows that I haven't been the best dad in the world. Volunteering to go to Iraq so many times, leaving Lisa alone with the kids, especially Katy. I don't know. I guess I didn't realize what I was doing to them, abandoning them like that. It's not like we needed the money, I've got more than enough to take care of us. I need to be a good father and be there for the kids. My father died when I was young, Ryan's age actually, and he wasn't what I'd exactly call a role model. Heavy drinking, betting on the horses, running around on my mom. That's not an excuse I know, and Lisa, honestly, I feel bad for Lisa. She tries hard, and she's a great person. But just not for me. What a mess!"

"Well, it isn't as though you intended to hurt anybody," I said. "You sound like you're being awfully hard on yourself."

"Not really," he said. "If I wanted to be brutally honest, I think I volunteered to get away from the hassle of the kids. Katy takes it out of me, watching that kid struggle to eat and breathe, can't walk, still in diapers. It's going to be that way forever. Ryan's temper was wearing on me, too—it got worse and worse. And Lisa's energy went to the kids and not me. Please don't get me wrong. I know the kids needed Lisa more than I did, and I was immature. People tell me I'm a hero for being in combat in Iraq, but I'm certainly no hero to Lisa."

I was thankful that Ryan arrived just then. Ryan sat down, folded his arms defiantly and said, "So, why is my dad here?"

"I'm here to help Mrs. G and Mr. M. explain to you why you need to go to a program that will help you do better in school," said Drew. "You need help Ryan, and everyone, including your mom, thinks that's the best thing to do for you right now. Get your grades up and behavior under control so you can go to any high school you want."

"I ain't goin' to no program and you can't make me."

"We'll try it for a while, see how it goes," said Drew. "I know it's the best thing to do, Little Man."

When his father said "Little Man," Ryan smiled broadly as though they shared an inside joke. But he was still having no part of it. "I don't want to go. I won't like the kids there. All the losers are in there. I'm no loser."

"No one's saying you're a loser," said Drew. "You were the man of the house while I was gone. Helping your mother with Katy. Mom said you were her hero."

Ryan raised his eyebrows as though he had never heard this news.

"Really? She said that?"

"I wouldn't lie about something so important to me. We both appreciate all that you did."

"How long do I have to stay?" Ryan asked.

"We're not sure Ryan," I said. "Usually it's as long as it takes to get things better. Till you get your grades up and your behavior is good enough so I don't worry about you. How's that?"

"OK, I guess. Dad, when do I start?"

"These fine people told me you'll begin Monday," said Drew. "After this weekend. I'll come back with you on the first day to meet your new teacher. What do you think?"

" OK, but I know I'm not going to like it."

"We'll just give it a try. How's that?"

Drew rose from his seat. It was a good idea for him to leave before Ryan had time to change his mind. Ryan walked with his dad to the door.

"See you Monday, and thanks for everything," Drew said.

Father and son, both heroes, turned and waved goodbye.

MY PERMANENT RECORD

Timmy pinned Jimmy to the floor. His breath was labored, as if he'd just run six miles in one hundred degree heat.

As soon as I spotted these two, in the seventh grade hallway, I yelled for them to stop immediately. Timmy jumped off Jimmy without hesitation, but Jimmy lay still with his eyes closed. No doubt Jimmy was humiliated.

I couldn't imagine what had provoked Timmy to attack Jimmy. Timmy was an excellent student and a polite and courteous young man. Jimmy was the class clown who'd once come to school with his eyebrows completely shaved.

I have to admit, I had a real soft spot for Jimmy's spunk and I knew that deep inside was a sensitive soul. I got a kick out of his red sneakers with matching red pants, and his hat with a spinner on the top. He was always the first to greet me when I had morning duty, and he loved sharing stories of his school bus escapades, or of relaxing with his dad on weekends. Rarely did a day go by without a visit from Jimmy.

One Valentine's Day, Jimmy handed me a pink envelope in the cafeteria. I asked if I could open it, but he said he'd preferred that I open it later. I couldn't wait to see what was inside. It is the rare seventh-grade boy who gives Valentine cards to his teacher, never mind the assistant principal. My card had pink carnations on the front and inside, Jimmy had written, "No one is as special as you. Love, Jimmy." The cynic in me thought it was a joke. But, then I remembered Jimmy's sensitive side and I realized it was the real deal.

I asked a coworker to take Jimmy to the nurse right away and turned my attention to Timmy. "So tell me, tough guy, what brings you to manhandle a fellow seventh- grader, wrestle him to the floor in front of all the other kids, and then sit there on top of him, gloating with satisfaction. Is this what your mother taught you? I know your mother and I think not."

Timmy was seated across from me and he was crying. His bottom lip quivered. He knew he was in big trouble. His mother was a math teacher in the school, and sure to hear of the incident very soon, if she hadn't already.

"Mrs. G.," Timmy could barely get the words out. He was having a tough time gathering his thoughts and I felt badly for the kid.

"Take a deep breath and just take your time. But tell the truth. You understand me? I want the truth. No baloney because you know I'm going to get Jimmy's side as well."

"Mrs. G, I'm going to tell the truth even though I need to say something that I know I shouldn't say in front of you. When I was climbing the stairs after lunch, Jimmy was ahead of me and he farted in my face."

It took me a few seconds to realize what he thought he wasn't supposed to say was 'farted.' I was prepared for something far worse but should have known because this was Timmy I was dealing with.

Well, now, that changed the situation a bit. This was pretty funny, the kind of story I share in the faculty room and at parties. I wanted to laugh out loud. But Timmy wasn't amused in the slightest.

Seventh-grade boys are probably the only demographic who think of farting in the face of another person, and actually act on their impulses. Teenagers have sex in cars. Seventh-grade boys fart in a classmate's face.

"I can see why you didn't like what Jimmy did," I said with as much gravity as I could muster. "But it's your reaction that has gotten you in trouble."

"I don't know why I did it," he said. "I just got so mad. You know how Jimmy is, always playing jokes, clowning around. My mother says he should go to a reform school. Am I suspended? Will this be on my permanent record? I'll never get into college if it's on my permanent record. Have I ruined my future? I've ruined my entire future, haven't I?"

Tears spilled down his face. I had never heard a seventh grader worry about his permanent record. His mother must have impressed upon him the importance of good behavior, and there was no doubt that he had internalized her words.

I couldn't let Timmy suffer for something any self-respecting seventh grade boy would have done without even thinking twice. But I also couldn't let Timmy get away with what amounted to an assault either.

"Timmy, you can't go around knocking people down when you don't like what they do. I understand that we have a special situation here with Jimmy's actions. The rules say I should suspend you for two days, but I don't want this on your permanent record either. So we need to make a deal. A secret deal because if you tell anyone, the deal is off."

Timmy was wide-eyed. "I want you to take a week of lunch detentions. You get in line first, no straggling, you get your lunch, you come to my office, and you sit. Five days. If I have to remind you, look for you, if you make extra work for me, the deal is off and you're out of here, suspended. Understand?"

"I understand, don't worry Mrs. G., I'll do it. Are you going to tell my mother?"

"That's up to you: if you mess up the deal, your mother gets the info. In fact, she has to if you're suspended. Get it? Now, here's a pass and git. Stay away from Jimmy—and his bodily functions."

I'm proud to say that Timmy kept up his end of our agreement. Thankfully, Jimmy wasn't hurt in the incident—but he had earned a few lunch detentions for his rude behavior. Fair is fair.

⟪―⟫

Fast-forward a few years. I ran into Timmy's mother at a party and she told me that Timmy had just graduated from high school and was off to engineering school. She also shared that on his last day at the high school, he stopped in at the office for one last check of his permanent record. She laughed.

"Is he *still* focused on that permanent record?" I asked.

She smiled. "Timmy told me about Jimmy and his flatulent activity a few years ago," she said. "He was anxious about what information was in the district's database and how it might affect his admission to a good school. It was silly, but he always worries about things like that. I'm glad you handled it the way you did. Poor Timmy was so nervous about being a good student and being a good boy that he would have made himself crazy if he had been suspended. So thanks for sparing the family a whole lot of grief."

You are welcome, dear parent. Thanks for giving me the opportunity to work with a student who is concerned with his future.

UNCLE JUAN

M aria was an eighth-grade student in my class for kids with behavior disorders. To my surprise, I discovered it was her aunt and uncle and not her parents, who were raising her in a crowded tenement, located just 200 yards from the school.

After several months of speaking on the phone, I finally met Maria's Uncle Juan when he came to pick her up for a medical appointment. His glasses were as thick as the proverbial coke bottles, and his Red Sox baseball cap left the tips of his ears exposed to the raw cold that November morning. A younger, long-legged man, whom he introduced as Kelvin, accompanied him.

"I legally blind but I drive with Kelvin," he explained in broken English. "He tell me when to stop and when to go," Juan said. "I no drive without Kelvin."

Juan went on to tell me that he was a minister in the local Pentecostal church, but that his time was largely taken up with fostering seven children, most of whom were relatives of extended family. In Puerto Rico, he had worked as a lineman for the phone company, but when his eyesight began to fail, he had to quit. After he lost his job, he contacted a cousin who lived in the United States who suggested that Juan come to live with him.

Chatting with Juan was like cozying up to a hot chocolate and a scone—he was warm-hearted, in spite of the stress at home. He was especially proud of taking a risk and leaving Puerto Rico, and I marveled at his ability to start over.

"I not know how I gonna live, but now with the foster children and my wife, she cook for the Spanish restaurant, we do OK."

"I give you credit for caring for seven foster children! Was Maria the first?" I asked.

"We get her when my wife niece, Jennie, go to party. She say, 'Can you babysit my daughter Maria? I be back after party.' But she not come back. Maria is two- year-old when Jennie go to party. So Maria, she stay with me now. She my daughter. She a little bossy I know, but she help me with the little kid at home. She cook for them, too."

"Maria seems to like the younger children here in the school," I said. "Looks like she's learned how to deal with them at home."

Speaking of Maria brought a smile to my face. She was a big girl, who often instigated altercations and intimidated some of the kids. I often had to call Juan to report what happened. But even though she could be ill tempered, I liked Maria because she was the champion of the underdog and when she caught bullies picking on smaller kids, she would fight for them. Bullies hit a nerve with her, even though some might have identified her as one.

"Oh, Maria a good girl," said Juan. "I know she a problem at school but what you gonna do? I say to my wife, 'Rosa, she come from bad seed. We gonna make a flower from the bad seed.' Maybe she like boys a lot now but we watch Maria, so she don' love them too much. Ha, like her mother."

Sure, people can discover cures for diseases, write the great American novel, and build a real estate empire, but who can parent seven foster children—at the same time—and still be so engaging and upbeat?

A small part of me felt ashamed. Teaching kids with behavior disorders wasn't making me joyous and my outlook on life was less than ten percent as bright as Juan's. The responsibility of trying to shape human beings who had suffered tremendous indignities like inadequate parenting, poverty, poor healthcare and a rundown broken school, was beginning to take its toll on me. I questioned my disciplinary methods and chastised myself when a lesson plan failed miserably. I believed that any lapse in judgment would surely contribute to the devastating ruin of my charges. And here stood Juan, believing that he was growing flowers from bad seeds. He was all about hope and faith. The man was a saint.

WHEN SMOKE GETS IN
YOUR EYES

When Jason fell in a puddle, I called his father to ask for a change of clothes. He not only wet his pants, he also wet the back of his shirt. The poor kid was freezing. I hurried Jason to the nurse's office so we could wrap him in blankets until his dad came with warm clothes.

We were able to reach Brian, Jason's dad, immediately. This was a man who took his parental obligations very seriously—Jason always had his homework completed and wore clean clothes.

Brian parked his truck in the handicapped spot, perhaps thinking that it was allowed because Jason was emotionally handicapped. With a cigarette locked between his lips, and wearing a dirty painter's cap and overalls, he rushed toward the school. I watched as he was stopped at the front door by Rollie, the safety officer, whom the kids ridiculed as "Rent a Cop." Rollie had been seated on a folding chair outside the front door. He rarely stood, citing a painful "bum leg" from childhood polio.

"No smoking allowed in the school," Rollie said with conviction, pointing to a tin can where Brian could extinguish the cigarette.

"Since when?" said Brian. "I been in this school with a butt before." Brian threw the cigarette to the ground and put it out with the toe of his work boot.

"Happy now 'Rent a Cop'?"

Rollie shook his head in disgust, and swung his legs to the right allowing Brian to pass.

The nurse's office was located next door to my classroom. After Jason had changed into fresh clothes, a very agitated Brian escorted him to the classroom.

"Ms. G, who is the person in the office downstairs?" he asked. "I saw her when I was coming up. I'm talking the fat-assed one with the brown hair. She was flappin' away down there on the phone with that loud voice. Is that the principal? Her name's not Mrs. Rappaport, is it?"

"Yes, that's Mrs. Rappaport. Why?"

"Man, she's still around? That old witch? I had her in second grade at the Donahue School and she was a mean bitch, pardon my French! I wasn't that smart in school and she sure didn't like me. If I had known she was here, I would have fought like hell to keep Jason out of this school. I don't care what they said about him stabbing that teacher with a butter knife, it was a bogus charge if you ask me. Give me a break."

"*You* had Mrs. Rappaport in second grade?" Jason said. "I pity you."

"And I pity you, tough guy! What's wrong with this city? Can't they get anybody decent to run this shithole? Oh I get it. An ass-hole is running a shithole, makes perfect sense."

I was stunned. He had a point but his foul language was unacceptable. Respect and relationships help make discipline effective and his kind of talk would not help our handling of Jason.

Joan had a tough job. She had to manage this abandoned parochial school, now taken over by the public sector because there was nowhere else to put six- hundred new students who arrived every school year from Puerto Rico and the Dominican Republic. The school had no gym, no cafeteria, no library and a bathroom with only one toilet stall for thirty-three staff members. Joan was no one that I wanted for a friend, but I did give her credit for holding the school together. Not to mention, she had very little support. No wonder she was prickly.

"I'm sorry for the language, I got carried away," said Brian, who had obviously gotten a good read of my disapproval. Brian seemed honestly contrite, and looked away toward Iris, my aide, to show that he was apologetic to her as well.

"You always talk like that, Dad," Jason said.

Brian rolled his eyes.

"Yeah, but I was wrong to do it in front of Ms. G and Ms. Moran."

I waited for some indication that he was planning to leave.

"Uh, Ms. G, can we talk in the hallway?"

Having a word with Brian was not something I looked forward to but I had no choice. He reeked of tobacco and I wanted to gag when he was close. But I sucked it up, held my breath, and nodded.

He hesitated when he shut the classroom door behind him, as though he didn't know where to begin. "I just want to give you some background on Jason, so maybe if he gets a little crazy, you can understand him better," he said. "He's a really good kid. I don't know if you know, but Jason is not my son. His mother was my girl-friend, she was a Dominican, that's why he's got that curly hair. I love him like he's my son. His brother, Brian, his half-brother that is, is mine and his mother's."

"Who is Jason's real father?" I asked.

"The guy was some white low-life, and he's a real jerk. There was another boy that those two had, Jason's mother and father, but he's dead. Murdered at two- years old by the father. Jason was four and witnessed the whole thing. The kid was slapped around for months and finally murdered. They found bruises all over him, a broken arm, finally he was slammed against the wall and he died of head injuries. His mother wasn't home when it happened but was found guilty of involuntary manslaughter, 'cause she had no direct role, just a sidekick role because she didn't do anything to stop the abuse."

Brian reached into his pocket for his cigarettes, but then thought better of it. "Oh yeah, no cigarettes. When I get nervous, the cigs calm me down and talking about this to you is making me nervous. Anyway." He patted his pocket to affirm they were still there.

"The guy was nuts," he went on. "And she was, too. Too drugged up to interfere or care. She spent some time in jail, in the women's prison. I started up with her after she got out and we had Brian together. He's four now, goes to the preschool over at the Y. She was a piece of work I'll tell you after that murder and prison and all, but her real problem is she's a crack head and I was no better, to be honest with you. She was clean in prison but she started right up after she got out. Couldn't wait, first day out. Then she started dealing and things were OK till she got caught. That's why she's back in jail."

This was a lot to digest. "I'm sorry for this Brian. Jason sounds like he's been through a lot."

"I'm trying to make it better, working at the paint company, trying to make an honest living instead of dealing drugs like I used to. I'm thirty-two years old, it's time to clean up my act a little, be responsible. But I'll tell you, it ain't easy when you've got the reputation that I've got."

I wondered if he had been in jail but I didn't want to ask. Anyway, I got the picture. As much as I now knew about Jason's situation, Brian didn't think it was enough. "I feel like the cops are watching me 24/7," he said. "A few weeks ago, they were looking for some druggie who lives next door. Jason didn't tell you about it? They busted into my apartment, flipped over the mattresses, pulled out all the drawers from the bureaus, opened my kitchen cabinets and threw cans and shit—oh, sorry—all over the place. Me and the boys were just sitting there, eating our hot dogs, watching TV, and they bust in like that. And then they're like 'Oh, sorry, we got the wrong apartment.' Then they go over and do the same thing to the guy next door. I should have reported them but what good would it do? The police in this town? They get away with murder. Literally. But no one believes it when it comes from someone like me."

After being in the city these last few years, it was hard to sympathize with anyone who might be thinking that he was getting a raw deal from the police. If the police were vindictive or paranoid, they had every right to be given the extensive drug dealing and robberies.

Still, I felt for Brian, trying to raise these two boys alone, both of whom were troubled. He didn't seem to have much money, given the ratty neighborhood where he lived, or the old beat-up truck he drove. He was doing his best. How could you not admire someone who takes a child in who's not even his own? A child who's been witness to a vicious murder? Whose mother has abandoned him? I didn't know many people who would do what Brian was doing. True, he was crass, disrespectful and smoked too much. But, I couldn't say that he wasn't doing a great job considering his circumstances. And I knew that Jason loved him.

"Thanks for sharing this with me," I said. "I'll keep it in mind when things get a little hairy. But so far, we've only had a few problems, which we've been able to work out. I like Jason."

"Yeah well, maybe you won't. Teachers start out liking him, and they end up hating him. And he hates them and then watch out. If he decides he hates you, he hates you. Kind of like your principal and me. I ain't never gonna like her. No way. But me? I love the kid and ain't no state agency gonna take him away from me. No friggin' way. "

"I'll try not to let it get to that point, this isn't a torture chamber," I assured him. "And Brian, thanks for being there for Jason. Where would he be without you?'

Brian got up to leave. He stuck his head into the classroom and yelled, "See you tonight, big guy. Be good!"

"Bye Dad!" Jason hollered back. "Don't forget! It's Sloppy Joe night!"

"IN *THIS* COUNTRY, BUSTER!"

The daytime janitor, Dave Brouillette, was in my classroom when I arrived. He was looking out into the schoolyard and beckoned for me to join him.

"See all those girls surrounding Carmen," Dave said. "I'll bet she's expecting a baby. I can tell by the way they're whispering and the girls stand real close. They've got a secret and they're protecting her. I've been with eighth graders a long time and I watch a lot. That girl is pregnant. I bet my right arm."

Carmen was one of my eighth-grade students. She was habitually truant, often strolling in after ten o'clock, only to immediately put her head down on her desk. When she did come to school on time, she would arrive ravenous.

"I'll send Carmen to the nurse today," I said. "I'll chat with the social worker about my concerns and your observations. They'll know what to do. I really hope it's not true."

I was worried about Carmen. She was only a child herself. But within the next few days, the nurse arranged for a clinic visit and confirmed that Carmen was five-months pregnant.

So now we knew what was ailing Carmen. It all made sense: the rounding of her belly, her disinterest in school, and the food she obsessed about. The nurse and social worker investigated the circumstances of the conception—if this pregnancy was the result of sexual assault or statutory rape, charges had to be made and the police needed to be involved.

Carmen confessed that the father was a friend of her mother's, a thirty-one-year old man with two children of his own, both in the Dominican Republic. Since the summer, they had been spending Saturday nights at a motel. The sick part of this, aside from the sex, was that Carmen's mother *knew* what was going on.

Joan, my principal, was livid when she heard the details and vowed justice. She arranged for the mother and her friend to meet in her office. My job was to be there as a witness, to keep notes, and to not say a word.

Gloria, the school interpreter, and I arranged the chairs so that we were off to the side. I hated these meetings because inevitably there would be raised voices, insults, innuendo and often crying and emotional outbursts. I didn't know if Joan created drama for drama's sake, but sometimes it appeared that way.

This would be the first time I had ever seen Carmen's mother, although I had heard a lot about her. I knew nothing of the friend. I hated this man and I hated this mother. They had ruined Carmen's future and had made a wreck of her childhood.

Carmen's mother, Cledianne, arrived first and seated herself next to Gloria. Her friend sat beside her. Cledianne was a stocky woman in her late twenties. Her blouse covered only one of her shoulders and her large hoop earrings hung almost to her collarbone. Her jeans were very tight and a roll of fat settled over the waistband like angel food cake rising over the top of a pan. Gang symbols were tattooed like a necklace around her neck. A soon to be grandmother. Delightful.

The friend was stocky as well. Even though it was winter, he had on baggy gym shorts and fancy sneakers with untied laces and he kept his sunglasses on. He also had diamond studs in both his ears.

"I'm told that neither of you needs a translator. Is that true?" Joan asked.

"Yes," Cledianne said, "I speak English and so does Nomar, but his English isn't so good so Gloria might need to help him."

Gloria nodded. Joan looked poised. "This is Mrs. Green, Carmen's teacher. She'll take notes and if there's time, she'll talk about how Carmen is doing in school. Ready to go?"

Everyone nodded in agreement. Ready to go.

"What brings us here today is that we have a very serious problem on our hands—all of ours—because Carmen, who is fourteen-years-old and a child herself is expecting a baby in four short months. There is no question that she needs to continue her education if she wants to have any future at all, and I will do everything in my power to see that that happens for her. But what I need to figure out today is how this pregnancy occurred and what you are going to do to make sure it doesn't happen again. So, tell me how *did* this happen? You are the mother? Yes? And you are Cledianne's friend? So what is your relationship to Carmen?"

"How do you know Carmen?" Gloria asked.

"Carmen, Cledianne daughter. I friend of both."

My pulse quickened.

"Carmen said that she has had sexual relations with you," said Joan. "Tell him that in Spanish, Gloria, so he knows exactly what I mean. And that she is having a baby and that she says you are the father."

Nomar was silent for what seemed an eternity. "Yes, I have the sex with her."

"Are you the father?" Joan asked gently. Nomar remained silent.

"Are you the father," she asked. "Answer me, don't go pretending like you don't know what I'm saying. And for heaven's sake, take off those foolish sunglasses. You look like a jerk. Of course you must be a jerk, if you're the father of a baby whose mother is fourteen years old!"

Nomar kept his sunglasses on.

"Yes, I the father," he responded.

"I had Carmen when I was fourteen and I'm doin' alright," said Cledianne. "I don't know why you're so mad about it. So she's pregnant, what do you care?"

"In my country…" Nomar began, but Joan cut him off.

"In *your* country? Are you *kidding* me? Don't you tell me about *your* country! You're in *this* country now, where people work and get an education! And in this country, we don't tolerate thirty-one-year-old guys screwing around with fourteen-year-old girls."

And in one of her classic moves, Joan lifted her oversized-body out of her chair, leaned over her desk, and put her face very close to Nomar's.

"In *this* country, buster, what you did is called statutory rape. Your lawyer can explain it to you, because once the police and I get done with you, your ass will be grass and you'll be parked in jail for a good long time. Count on it because the two of you are scumbags of the worst order. Now get the hell out of here before I kill you both."

Nomar and Cledianne got up simultaneously and couldn't get to the door fast enough.

"Fuck you, bitch!" Nomar shouted.

"Yeah, fuck you, bitch," said Cledianne.

Gloria and I were speechless. Joan leaned back, folded her arms tightly across her chest and said, "Do you believe those fucking scumbags? Acting like this is normal behavior? God, ruining kids' lives."

Amen, Joan. Amen.

Nomar later appeared before a judge who gave him a choice: Return to the Dominican Republic or spend one and a half years in the County House of Correction. Nomar chose deportation. Carmen gave birth to a healthy baby boy in the spring and returned in the fall to begin high school.

PARKY POO

It was five past two in the afternoon and the phone in my office was ringing off the hook. School had been out for twenty minutes already, long enough for Parker to arrive home to tell his mother, Laura, all about another miserable day in sixth grade.

Based on the events of the day, I knew I shouldn't answer. We had dealt with an emergency evacuation—of eleven hundred kids—because someone had written "Time to Kill, See You at 10:30" in lipstick on the girls' restroom mirror and two eighth-grade girls had engaged in a hair-pulling fight over a newly-enrolled male student with a tattoo.

I was certain that Laura was aware of these incidents. She knew about everything that went on because she was an avid school volunteer who spent time in the parking lot, the office, the cafeteria and the library. We all knew that she was gathering information to use as ammunition against anyone whom she believed was messing with Parker's well being.

I eventually answered the phone. If I hadn't, she'd assume that I was avoiding her—which, of course, was true.

"Mona? Laura! Well, it's been another one of those days for my Parky Poo. I am done, done, done with your school. Parky has come home every single day in the last two weeks, sick to his stomach. I see him dragging his poor, pitiful self through my front door, his eyes downcast, and I want to burst into tears. Can you imagine what it feels like to be a mother, seeing your baby son like that? You're a mother. Could you stand it?"

I felt as though I had just hit the replay button. Didn't I have this very same conversation yesterday and the day before that?

"Help me to help you, Laura. Give me some specifics so I can see if we can come up with some solutions."

"You and those other jamokes on the staff won't help my Parky. Instead, you're all making things worse. I am seeing a happy, self-confident fifth grader turn into a defeated sixth grader and we're only in the fifth week of school. He hates everything about your place. Everything. Do you understand? And don't think for a moment that everyone in town isn't going to know about the misery that my Parky Poo is experiencing. I know a lot of people, Mona. A lot of people."

"Laura, I want to help you but right now I don't know what you want. Give me something to work with. Please."

Laura loved this. It was her chance to shine. "You better not be telling me to talk this over with Henry. You call him a school psychologist? What kind of a school psychologist tells a parent that she is *too* involved, in so many words. Then he tells me that Parky is able-bodied enough to do his homework alone. Are you kidding me? The kid has a twenty-percent hearing loss in his right ear. Doesn't he know that Parky Poo had a serious kidney infection when he was two years old? I'll tell you what happened today. He came home, very upset because, once again, no one would sit with him at lunch. Do you know how humiliating that is for a kid? To be alone at a lunch table?"

This wasn't true. I had watched Parker in the lunchroom and he was seated with a bunch of sixth-grade boys. What I wanted to say was, "Laura, you need to get a life. Every day you waste twenty minutes of my time, complaining about problems that you manufacture for what reason, I don't know. After 180 days of school, I will have spent sixty hours listening to your stories, which you have been repeating since your son began kindergarten. You are ruining your son and turning him into a cry baby that makes him red meat for every middle school bully in town."

Instead, I said, "Laura, I'm in the cafeteria every day with Parker and I make a point of making sure that he is not eating alone. He may be alone for a few minutes when other kids run up to get ice cream, but he doesn't eat alone. Trust me."

I knew that Laura would challenge me. She'd launch into this fray with the gusto of a four-year-old chasing pigeons in the park. To be frank, I would have welcomed a mild heart attack just to get away from her.

"Are you calling my Parky Poo a liar? I know my kid and my kid don't lie. If he says that he's eating alone, he's eating alone. He says that kids move away from him when he sits down, and they don't listen when he talks. I saw this myself when I went into the cafeteria to observe what really goes on down there. The kids I saw were rude, worse than rude. And what are you doing to change that behavior? You and all those so-called educators who don't know their ass from their elbow? You're telling me that he's only alone when the kids get their ice cream? Are you kidding me?"

I knew she was wrapping things up because she had insulted most of the staff and me—that was her pattern. But just in case, I gave Kathy, the school secretary, our private Laura signal. I twirled my finger around the side of my head so Kathy could alert me to the arrival of my fictitious 2:30 appointment.

"Laura, I'll make sure that the sixth grade teachers are aware of your concerns and I'll continue to monitor Parker in the lunchroom. I'll chat with the adjustment counselor tomorrow as well. Kathy, what? Oh, they're here? I'm sorry, Laura, but I've got to go and meet with some parents. Pretty important. I'm sure you understand. Call me if you have other concerns."

I'm a phony, but I knew she'd be back at it a little after two o'clock the next day. And I'd be there; listening, commiserating, stroking and getting nowhere.

And I knew it wasn't really about Parky Poo.

PREMIER JANITORIAL SERVICES

Whenever I called Wilfredo, I thought I was calling the owner of Premier Janitorial Services. A recorded message announced that "Mr. Gonzales is not in the office at this time. Please leave a name and phone number." I always cooperated with the recording except that Wilfredo never phoned back.

The calling went on for days, and I'm sure he assumed that I was some whiny school administrator complaining about his spirited son, Oscar, a new sixth-grader. I wasn't calling to complain. I needed him to give us permission to evaluate Oscar because the teachers suspected a learning disability.

Wilfredo finally popped into my office during the last week of the summer while I finalized the seventh-grade schedules. He was round-faced and his tan pants were painted with oil stains. A pencil rested comfortably above his ear.

"You been looking for me," he said. "I in the neighborhood doin' some work and I tink to myself, 'Dat lady gonna come after me real good if I don't talk to her.' I get your las' call and I know you mean business!"

I immediately liked Wilfredo. I knew that he was showboating, but I could forgive a hard-working single parent who was preoccupied with making a living in a new country. It's not easy clawing your way to what everyone else takes for granted or thinks is his due.

I explained what I needed and gave Wilfredo some information to read.

"No paper, I no read Ingles. I know you do da right ting for Oscar. I sign for you now. I need to go to work." Wilfredo scribbled his signature in a hurry and then apologized for running out. I can't say that Wilfredo returned phone calls promptly after we'd finally met. However, he'd typically call back at some point, usually after we had solved a crisis without him.

One winter morning, I arrived to school way later than usual and got caught up in the drop-off mess in the school driveway. Just ahead of me I spied a steel grey Hummer trying to worm its way around a few cars to get to the entrance faster. It was Wilfredo. He was unsuccessful, so he backed into his original spot. When he braked in front of the cafeteria entrance, Oscar tumbled out of the Hummer and gave his father a dismissive wave.

After I parked and completed my morning supervision, I poked my head into Oscar's classroom to check on him, and the teacher told me he was MIA. I guessed that he was in the principal's office, but after ten minutes, that seemed unlikely. I was worried and called the school secretary, Deb, to ask about Oscar's whereabouts.

"You didn't hear?" said Deb. "His father was killed at 7:30 this morning. Dropped off Oscar, went home to get his fourth grader, and he was shot in the head in his driveway. Too early to tell what this is about but somebody said Mr. Gonzales was involved with drugs. A nice man like that. Can you imagine? We have Oscar here with one of the counselors waiting for his aunt to pick him up."

I thought about Wilfredo's fourth-grade daughter, the tiny Jessenia, whom I met one day after school when Wilfredo pulled up to the designated pick-up area of the school. She was licking an ice cream cone and her dog in the backseat was trying to sneak in a few licks. Had she seen her father murdered? Was she hurt as well? Where was she?

⬥

The newspapers reported the story. Murders like this were rare in the town. There was speculation about what Wilfredo did for a living given that he drove a Hummer and was gunned down by an automatic weapon in broad daylight. He had been arrested in the 80's for drug trafficking, and there had been a few arrests since that time, but his record of the last fifteen years was clean.

I was incensed by the coverage. I felt that the reporting was long on speculation and short on facts. It was so embarrassing for the children and I grieved for Oscar and Jessenia who were now fatherless and had to deal with the rumors about their father's alleged sordid activities. What a mess.

The wake was held in a neighboring city, in a funeral home across the street from the large Catholic Church that had once served the Irish faithful. It was a cold, dark, rainy evening on the night I paid my respects. The funeral home was a tired building that needed a fresh coat of paint. I hoped that Oscar and Jessenia didn't notice how dreary and depressing the place was.

I saw Oscar in the distance and I waded through mobs of young people, most speaking softly in Spanish. He was standing beside a woman whom I assumed to be his Aunt Estephany. The counselors at school described her as a kind, God-fearing woman with three, grown children who would now be caring for him and Jessenia.

Oscar stiffened when I gave him a quick hug. I told him how sorry I was about Wilfredo. Oscar nodded. It wasn't until I released him that I noticed the phalanx of men standing behind Wilfredo's open casket. There were five of them, all dressed in black leather jackets, backward baseball hats and black sunglasses. Their arms were folded across their chests. I bowed my head and asked God to be merciful, maybe cut Wilfredo a little slack.

I couldn't wait to get out of there. From the looks of the tough guys standing guard, it seemed like trouble was expected.

For months, I perused the newspapers searching for news of Wilfredo's assailant. There was no more news about the murder, so I had no idea if any of the rumors had been true. But I did know that he was a good dad.

Rest in peace, Wilfredo Gonzales.

SEX TEACHER

Eighth graders spend a lot of time thinking and talking about sex. You can be a geek, Goth, jock or brainiac. Your face can be coated with pimples, you can be six-feet tall and weigh ninety pounds, or barely able to squeeze your ample bum into a classroom seat. It doesn't matter. If you're an eighth grader, you're interested in sex.

When Lauren came into the special education office to discuss the budding romance of her eighth-grade students, Matthew and Crystal, I wasn't surprised. Her classroom had eight students with cognitive impairments, and two of them were these lovebirds. She said they insisted on sitting together for every classroom activity and at a private table in a secluded corner of the cafeteria.

"What do you expect?" I asked her. "That's what eighth graders do, they fall in love. Just because the minds of the two kids in question are a little delayed, it doesn't mean their bodies are."

Matthew possessed the engaging peculiarities that make children with Down Syndrome so much fun to be around. He told jokes with perfect timing, and even though he told the same three jokes over and over again, I never tired of them. I looked forward to his impromptu visits to my office to show me his "table" and "downward dog" yoga poses. Despite my chiding him to knock before entering, and to greet me with a hello, he insisted on barging in and getting right down to business with his yoga performance.

Crystal was adopted when she was a five-year-old by a middle-aged couple, Jeannie and Ernie, who had married late and wanted a family. Her biological family was guilty of ravaging her with every abuse imaginable, but somehow Crystal's personality emerged unscathed. She possessed no malice or resentment and was open to new experiences and challenges. She did have a mild cognitive impairment that impeded her academic performance, and she was also diagnosed with an obsessive-compulsive disorder. She occasionally stole things from CVS and became very agitated when there was a change in her routine that occurred without warning. Crystal was a frequent visitor to my office, typically to give me a hand-drawn picture of flowers or animals to hang in my gallery of student artwork.

Matthew and Crystal's romance blossomed with nightly phone calls at seven o'clock. They rehashed what happened during the school day and Matthew imitated his favorite TV characters. Crystal's parents began to use a timer to set a limit on the length of their phone calls, but that only encouraged Matthew to call again later to finish all that he had to say. Soon, Matthew was calling three and four times per night.

We began to have our fair share of difficulties at school, too. The school had a "hands off" policy, which Lauren spent a large amount of time explaining and reviewing. Despite the daily tutelage on the handbook's policies, Matthew and Crystal ignored them. Rarely did a day go by that I didn't receive reports of Matthew and Crystal holding hands while walking down the hall, hugging and kissing under the stairways.

Although Matthew seemed to be the more smitten of the two, it was clear that their relationship was escalating. All we needed was a pregnant eighth grader on our hands.

Both sets of parents called to express concern and suggested it was time for a sexual education program. We didn't have a staff member who was equipped to handle the job, which required an understanding of how to teach people with cognitive impairments along with knowledge of the subtleties of sexual relationships and sexual functioning. And there was no money in the budget.

We continued to monitor and counsel, and one afternoon Mr. Spano, the assistant principal, startled me while I was enjoying a quick lunch behind the closed door of my office

"Sorry to bother you, but Matthew and Crystal were just caught with their pants down in the cafeteria. They're with Lauren right now."

My fork stopped halfway to my mouth. How was I going to explain this to their parents? They managed to get their pants down in the cafeteria? Did any kids see them? How long were their pants down? Now it was my turn to interrupt someone's lunch.

Joe had been on cafeteria duty and was now in the teacher's lunchroom guzzling a Diet Coke when I tracked him down. He was a no-nonsense guy with a direct approach.

"I'm assuming you're here because you were clued you in about our very own Romeo and Juliet?" Joe reached for his popcorn and shoved a handful in his mouth.

"From what I heard, Joe, I'm going to have lot of 'splainin to do to the parents of those two. Especially Crystal's parents. They are very threatened by this romance, so tell me what happened. Every damn detail. They'll want that."

"Well, I was standing in the middle of the cafeteria, directing kids at their tables to the lunch line. There was the usual ruckus, kids knocking into kids to get in line. You know the drill. Usually I call Matthew and Crystal first, to keep them busy with food and not each other. But I was distracted today, there was a lot going on. Anyway, I remembered them after all the other kids had gotten their lunches.

OK, so I'm looking around the cafeteria to make sure that I didn't miss anybody, and lo and behold there are Crystal and Matthew looking under the table. I wondered what they were looking at, of course, and walked toward them. They apparently didn't notice when I got to the table, and when I crouched down to see what was so interesting, I saw that they both had their pants—and their underpants, mind you—pushed down to their knees. They looked at me in shock and scurried to pull up their pants."

"God help us," I said. "You come to school in the morning and you never know what you're going to find! How do you prepare for this? Anyway, then what happened?"

"Matthew said, 'I didn't have my pants down!' And Crystal said, 'Me either.' So I said, 'Then what were you doing?' 'I was showing Crystal what I have in my pockets,' said Matt. 'And I was showing

Matthew what I have in *my* pockets,' Crystal said. Give them credit for being quick on the uptake."

"So then you sent them to Lauren's classroom. And what did she do?"

"Probably didn't buy the pocket story, if I know her. But really, can you blame them for wanting to see each other's body parts? Every kid wants to see that right? And where are they going to see that stuff? Those two are always supervised by some adult, never having any private time that I know of, right? I give them credit for almost getting away with it."

"Thanks for your input, but really, we need to keep a closer eye on them. This is beyond the beyond."

⚔

Crystal's dad, Ernie, was appalled when I called to give him the news.

"What kind of a circus are you people running over there? How on God's green earth can someone with Matthew's capacity get away with pulling down his pants and showing my innocent daughter his family jewels? I can't believe this nonsense."

Things didn't go much better with Matthew's mother. "All Matthew knows about his penis is that he pees with it. He doesn't know about sex. Crystal put all these rotten ideas in his head. This is embarrassing for my whole family. And what are *you* going to do about this?"

That was a good question.

The principal and I decided to have Matthew and Crystal escorted whenever they left the classroom so that they never were alone with each other and never, ever unsupervised. I was still working out the logistics when Ernie called a few days after the incident. I knew that he was a conscientious parent, and I admired him for adopting a child like Crystal, who was anything but easy to raise. But a charm school graduate he wasn't. He said whatever he pleased. The filter that was missing from his cigarettes was also missing from his mouth. "I don't suppose you people have found that sex teacher you was looking for, am I right?" he said.

"No, no we haven't Ernie. No money, no teacher. Maybe next year. I'm hoping anyway. Maybe we can get someone trained this summer, but I'm not holding my breath."

"I was thinkin' of volunteerin' to be a sex teacher for you. I think I could do a decent job given all the life experiences I have in that department." He laughed and I hoped that he knew he was being ridiculous. "But the missus says you're probably not all that interested in what I have to say about sex, and I'm guessing she's right."

"I think your wife is thinking clearly," I agreed.

"Well, alright then," he chuckled. "Seriously now, me and the missus are sellin' my truck soon. We got no need of it. We figure we can get at least a couple thousand for that truck. It's a 1999 but it only has seventy thousand miles on it. Maybe we'll get more. Who knows? We'll give whatever we get to the school to pay for a sex ed teacher, that is, if you want it."

Now this was a welcome surprise. I thanked Ernie profusely for his generous offer and told him that I would discuss it with the principal.

"Now don't you go blabbin' about this all over town. I want everyone to think that I'm poor and crabby so they won't come 'round botherin' me about givin' to this cause and helpin' out that cause. This is between you and me and that good lookin' principal of yours. Do we have a deal, sunshine?"

"Yes, Ernie, we've got a deal!"

Sex teacher paid for by anonymous donors, Ernie and the Missus. Not in my wildest dreams.

THERE'S NO ONE ELSE LIKE ME

There was something going on with Chedeline and I couldn't figure out what it was. She was extremely quiet and barely passing. I had been watching her closely, looking for signs of bullying even.

Maybe something had happened at home or in Haiti with her grandparents. Her parents both worked two jobs and Chedeline had a lot of responsibility as the oldest of five—every day after school she cooked dinner, helped the younger kids with homework and did laundry. She was most likely exhausted and overwhelmed.

Chedeline had emigrated from Haiti when she was in the fifth grade. She kept her hair short and she had lovely ebony skin. She had a younger sister, Fabiola, in the seventh grade who was a little smaller than she. They seemed to share what little clothes they had.

Chedeline rarely smiled or laughed.

"It's OK to laugh, Chedeline," I said on occasion, typically when her peers and I were laughing about something that was legitimately funny.

"I'm here to learn not laugh," she once told me.

Chedeline was the stuff of teacher fantasies. She completed assignments on time and asked thoughtful questions. She excelled in math, which is what led the team of teachers to place her in a high-level math class. Chedeline was able to grasp complex concepts quickly.

I was baffled by Chedeline's recent behavior and she wasn't living up to her potential. This was a crucial year—high school placements were based on eighth-grade achievement. Poor performance might affect her plans for high school and whether she went to college on scholarship. As a poor immigrant, she needed to know that. She didn't have well-connected or savvy parents to help her to navigate her future. We were all she had and we had a huge responsibility to help as best we could.

One day, I asked Chedeline if she would join me for lunch.

"Will there be only me?" she asked. I couldn't tell if she wanted to be alone or if she wanted someone else to be with her.

"Of course," I said. "I'll order pizza, or subs, whatever you like and we can chat about whatever you want." She agreed.

I knew she would be anxious—Chedeline didn't like special attention from adults, nor did she enjoy being singled out for her accomplishments. She was emotionally self-contained and relentlessly driven to achieve. I wondered if Chedeline had secrets that might have explained her unwillingness to emote, the kind that make you say, "So *that's* why...."

We met as planned in my classroom—Greek salad for me, meatball sub for Chedeline. She removed the sub from the bag and laid it horizontally in the middle of the paper wrap. She folded the napkin in her lap. I opened my can of soda and began to eat. Chedeline watched me.

"Chedeline, please, eat," I said.

"I'm not hungry," she said.

"What do you mean? Of course, you're hungry. You haven't eaten since you left your house this morning. What time was that? Seven? It's noon and you're thirteen-years-old. Of course you're hungry."

"I'm not hungry, Miss."

"Did you eat at home when you got up in the morning?"

"Lately, I'm just not so hungry. I don't know why."

"How long has this been going on? That you're not hungry? That's not normal for someone your age, Chedeline. Is something bothering you, making you too upset to eat?"

"Not really. I don't know. Everything is fine at home. My parents work a lot but that's been going on since we moved here."

"What about at school? Are you happy here?"

"Sometimes."

"Which sometimes are you not happy?"

Silence.

"Chedeline, can you tell me about the times when you are not happy?"

"In my math class," she said.

"What bothers you about math class?"

"I'm the only black student in the class."

What? We practically had the United Nations in that class. There were kids from the Dominican Republic, Thailand, Albania, Portugal and Ecuador. What was she talking about?

"Chedeline, there are other kids of color in that class. I'm confused. What about all of your classmates from the Dominican Republic?"

She sighed. "They're not black, Miss. They're brown. There's no one else like me. I'm the only *real* black person in the class." She folded her hands back into her lap. "I want to get out of there and be with other people like myself."

"But you won't be with the highest math achievers where you belong. No one in your class notices that you have black skin. Do they? How could they? Everyone is a different color in there and no one cares."

"*I* care and I want to get out. Please, Ms. G, get me out. I don't want to be the only real black person in the class."

Chedeline finally made eye contact with me.

"Chedeline, I feel terrible about what you're saying and I'm sorry that you feel that way. But once you get to know all the kids in there, you'll see, you won't even be thinking about color."

"Yes, I will. You don't understand because you're not black. I'm not comfortable in there with all the kids looking at me because I'm *too* black. "

She was right. Maybe I didn't understand, but it seemed to me that there was more to this.

"Has anyone been mean to you? Has anyone made you feel uncomfortable because you're black? Are any boys bothering you in any way?"

"No, Miss. No one is bothering me. Not like you think. But I know the teacher thinks I'm dumb because I'm black, *real* black. She makes me nervous, the way she explains things like she would to a dumb person, all slow like I can't hear. I *can* hear. I don't see her doing that to anyone else. And I'm not dumb."

I had a hunch that Chedeline was telling the truth. When asked to answer a question or to explain a concept, Chedeline often took her time to respond.

"You think she talks to you slowly because you're black? Not because she's trying to help you understand?"

"Miss, I'm not crazy. She thinks I'm dumb because I'm black. And when she acts like that, everyone looks at me, and feels bad for me because I know that they're thinking, 'I'm glad I'm not as black as her.' You think I'm crazy too, don't you? But you don't go in the ladies' room and have the hall monitor follow you even though she was walking in the other direction, or go in Sauve's Market and watch the man behind the counter not take his eyes off you because he thinks you're going to steal. I don't steal. I don't stuff paper in toilet. But everybody thinks I do because I'm black. It's not easy being black."

I realized that despite Chedeline's remarkable resiliency, she was trying to maneuver in a society that was not only foreign, but also unforgiving and hostile. None of this should have been news to me.

"Chedeline, how would being in a class with other 'real black' kids help you?"

"I wouldn't be alone like I am now. No matter how many kids are in the class, I am alone. There would be other kids who understand me, even if they weren't my friends. I don't like being alone at all."

I was proud of her for advocating for herself. She was so vulnerable at this tender age, trying to make her way into a society that made no sense to her, but expected her to make sense of it. It was my turn to advocate for her.

"Chedeline, nobody wants to be alone in a classroom. I don't blame you at all. I'll talk to the other teachers and we'll see what we can do."

"Thanks, Miss G. If you move me, I promise I'll do the best that I can. I won't let you down." Chedeline finally took a bite of her sub. "I'm hungry now," she confessed through a mouthful of meatball. "I don't know why."

We did move Chedeline to a class with other "real black" students. She aced that class. No surprise.

YOU SHOULD BE ASHAMED

One rainy fall day, I sought out Gloria, the elementary school adjustment counselor, for some advice about how to deal with Javier, a fifth-grader who had stolen my cellphone. Gloria's office was one of those pseudo offices with only half walls, so anyone who walked by or stood nearby was privy to her confidential conversations—and vice versa.

It hadn't taken a skilled sleuth to figure out that Javier had stolen my phone. Within five minutes of leaving school for the day, he'd called his mother's number and made thirty-seven calls within the next twenty-four hours. The phone company sent me a printout of the calls as soon as I reported the phone missing.

Javier didn't deny what he had done. He'd even written an apologetic note, begging me to forgive him and insisting that he would never steal again. Only a fool would have believed his promises, but I did want to forgive him. After all, he had returned my phone.

Kim, the school secretary, had a good view from her desk of the hallway stairs, and she loved to give play-by-plays of the activity outside of the office. "Hey, your boyfriend Josue is coming up the stairs, in case you want to know," she shouted to Rick, the parent liaison in the next office.

"That little shit. Every day, he's late," Rick shouted back.

When Josue had reached the top of the stairs, Rick was there to greet him. Josue was dressed in a white-collared polo shirt stained with spaghetti sauce and navy blue pants that were several sizes too big for his fifty-pound frame. "You come right this way young man," said Rick. "It's 9:30? You're an hour-and-a-half late. A quarter of the day is gone. Do you know that? Do you?"

Gloria and I didn't hear Josue respond, but I was certain that he knew he was late.

"Why bother coming in at this hour?" Rick yelled in his face, much louder than was necessary. They stood on the other side of the wall, oblivious to the fact that Gloria and I could hear their conversation. It occurred to me that Rick had also been listening to my conversation with Gloria about Javier and my cellphone. I didn't like Rick at all, especially the harsh way he treated the kids in the school.

"He has Josue, "Gloria whispered. "The new third grader."

"I think I know Josue," I said. "Is his brother Javier?"

"Yes, but Javier lives with the dad. Josue lives with the mom."

I knew a lot about this family.

Rick had just been warming up. "Why are you late every single day," he said. "Don't you have an alarm clock? You're old enough to have an alarm clock! You're how old? Nine? You should be able to set an alarm clock and arrive at school on time. Aren't you ashamed of yourself?"

Aren't you ashamed of yourself? I had heard that before. I was a fifth-grader at St Marguerite's School. My classmate, Elaine Duquette, stood in front of the class, waiting for Sister Rose to give her a fraction problem to solve at the blackboard. Sometimes three students at a time would go up, to save time—there were almost 50 kids in the class. For some reason, Sister Rose sent Elaine up to the board alone this time. She surely knew that Elaine was one of the slowest learners in the class—we all did.

The problem involved adding fractions with different denominators. As expected, Elaine didn't find a common denominator and instead added the denominators as they were, which of course, was wrong.

Sister stood near the first row where the smart kids sat. She was right beside me and the big black beads of her rosary hung so low from her belt that I was afraid they would catch on my hand if I let my arm hang by my seat. I was thinking about how she prayed to God's beloved Son with those rosary beads, big as Concord grapes, in her fat fingered hands when her sharp voice startled me into paying attention.

"That's wrong!" she snapped at Elaine. "Don't you know how to add those two fractions together? We've been working on this for three days. What's wrong with you?"

Elaine stood paralyzed. "She always gets it wrong," one of the boys yelled from the back of the room.

"Look at me," Sister Rose said to Elaine. "Did you do your homework last night?"

Elaine looked up into her eyes. "No, Sister."

"Why not?"

"I didn't know how to do it."

"What do you mean, you didn't know how to do it? Are you dumb? Wasn't anyone there who could help you? Your father? Your mother?"

"They were both working and I was alone with my baby brother. I was babysitting him."

"You know that's a lie. I don't believe you for one minute."

I knew it was the truth because I lived across the street. I wanted to say, "I know she's telling the truth" but I knew it would make things worse.

The class was silent.

Suddenly, a stream of urine trickled down Elaine's leg and a small puddle formed on the floor. She blinked repeatedly but otherwise didn't move.

"Look at that *grand bebe va*," Sister Rose said. "Get yourself to the bathroom right now, and on your way, find Mr. Robideau and tell him we need him to clean your mess up. You should be ashamed of yourself." We were French Canadian kids and we all knew that *grand bebe va* meant wicked big baby, the worst insult a fifth grader could get.

Elaine covered her eyes and rushed out of the classroom. I fought to hold back my tears. How would she ever have the courage to return to face her classmates and Sister Rose?

It didn't make any sense to me that someone should be ashamed of something that wasn't her fault. That was my fifth grade thinking. Elaine was a slow learner and I couldn't understand why a grown adult would be so mean-spirited to someone so ill equipped to fight back.

I continued to sit in Gloria's office listening to Rick go at Josue. "So you're lazy and just can't get out of bed, am I right, tell me I'm right," he yelled. Rick wasn't letting up. I wanted to leave Gloria's office and slam Rick to the floor.

"I try to get up when my mother calls me, but I just go back to sleep," said Josue.

"Just admit that you're lazy. Admit it."

"He's making me sick. I can't stand any more of this!" I whispered to Gloria. I got up, opened the door and stood face-to-face with Rick.

"Enough, Rick!" I said. "Josue, let me give you a pass and you can tell your teacher that you were with me and the counselor. You're OK, you're OK. Go on up."

Josue grabbed the pass and left the room as fast as he could. I was now alone with Rick. I looked him up and down. He looked at me, waiting. He didn't appear to be embarrassed because he was caught bullying this poor little guy. Instead, the read I got, was that he was proud, smug and arrogant.

"Not for anything," I sneered, "but you are a major, major ass-hole. You have no right to yell at a kid like that. Your job is to call his parent if he is late, not to get on his case. He is nine years old. His mother just got her first real job after working the streets to make a living. She leaves the house at six in the morning. No wonder the kid goes back to bed. Do you think that you were getting yourself up for school in third grade? Your wife is probably getting you up now for all I know. Truly, you are a merciless coward. You don't belong in a school, Rick; you belong in a cave where you can't hurt anybody. Do you hear me? You belong in a cave."

My heart was beating faster and faster and I knew it was time to quit before someone called the police. God, I hated adult bullies and here was one in living color, standing right in front of me.

Rick didn't say a word. And he didn't move. "And don't expect an apology from me buster!" I said. "If I ever hear you yell at a kid like that again, let me tell you, you can expect a lot worse. You haven't seen anything yet. And that's no threat. I mean it."

It was my turn to escape like Josue did, but unfortunately for me, I had no pass.

WE'RE DOING QUITE WELL,
THANK YOU

I heard the news on my way to work at the middle school. Duc Pham, forty-seven years old, had flung himself over an overpass on Route 73 at four thirty in the morning.

Pham was a popular Vietnamese name, and I didn't realize until I arrived at school that it was the same Mr. Pham I had known, the father of two of our students, one in eighth grade, and one in sixth grade. The school secretary told me that Mrs. Pham had called earlier that morning to report her children's absence.

I vaguely knew Huy, the eighth grader. He was a good student who caused no trouble. He was taller than most Vietnamese boys, and very polite. His friends were serious, well-behaved students as well.

Lien, his sister in the sixth grade, was petite and delicate, and liked to giggle and spend time with her friends. She was also a solid A student. I couldn't imagine Lien getting caught up in Facebook drama or stealing boyfriends from precocious twelve year olds.

As the school's assistant principal, I wanted to pay my respects to the family and attend Mr. Pham's wake. Through the years, I attended several wakes for parents of my middle school students who had unexpectedly died like Mr. Pham. When I arrived at the funeral home, I joined the long line of mourners that had snaked around the south side of the building, mostly middle-aged and elderly Vietnamese people who were silent and expressionless during the hour it took to reach the front door.

Once inside, I signed the guest book, which was on table next to a makeshift altar that had a framed picture of Mr. Pham, as well as several lacquered bowls of cooked rice and small melons. There were several ceramic urns on each side of the photo, and white votive candles flickered beside little sprays of yellow roses and greens in glass vases. And elderly man lit some incense, and bowed with folded hands. I also bowed.

I made my way to the main room where a dozen or so people surrounded Huy, Lien, and the woman I assumed to be their mother. Long white bands of cloth were tied around their heads which the funeral director later informed me signified that they were the chief mourners in the group. I approached the open casket to kneel and say a few prayers. The room was eerily silent. I thought of the time many years ago when I had opened the *Evening News* and read an article about a local woman who was discovered dead in her car in a parking lot by police. I read that it appeared that she had taken her own life, although there was no mention of how. She was forty-seven years old. I knew this woman, and I was very distressed by this news. I had spoken to her several weeks' prior at my daughter's high school graduation. We'd known each other for years, usually meeting up at school events. We were not close but we would sometimes chat about how difficult it could be to raise a daughter. Her last words to me were, "Everything has a price", and I wondered what price her family was paying for her suicide. My sister, Linette had called just as I had finished reading the sad news and I told her about what happened. Linette was dying of cancer,and I had been in denial for a long time. "Here's this woman," she said," who takes her own life, when I would give anything to keep mine."

After I finished praying in front of Mr. Pham's casket, I glanced over at the Pham family, unsure if I should approach them to express my condolences or continue on my way. I had seen no one else in this sea of mourners reach out to them. Mrs. Pham, perhaps sensing my awkwardness, rose from her chair and walked toward me. Lien and Huy followed close behind. She took my hand into a soft warm grasp as her children stood behind her. It was obvious that she did not know who I was, and before I could introduce myself, she turned her head and looked at Huy with her eyebrows raised.

"It's Mrs. Green, from the school," Huy said.

"Oh yes. You are the first to come here. Huy and Lien love your school and Duc and me, we are so proud of them there."

I marveled at how composed and gracious she was under the circumstances. Maybe her reality hadn't sunk in yet; she still used the present tense when she mentioned her husband.

"I'm awfully sorry for your loss, Mrs. Pham," I said. "Your life will change quite a bit, I'm sure, and I want you to know that the school staff is prepared to help you in any way that you need."

"Yes, thank you," she said. "It is quite a surprise that we have here. Duc worried a lot about his business and I guess he worried too much. Me, I think he is in a better place. It's not good to worry all the time, eat only a little bit, sleep only a few hours every night. He made himself crazy even though I tried to tell him, 'Duc, it's only business, it's only business.' He worried about paying his bills, making new business, customers getting mad at him. What can I say? I tried to help him, but he said that I couldn't help him. He was a difficult man to reach, and I could sense that he was getting more and more desperate, more agitated. But I never imagined this, him leaving us without saying goodbye. Leaving the house while I was asleep." Mrs. Pham's voice softened. "His worry is over now. Forever."

I imagined Mr. Pham sneaking out of the house, closing the door very carefully not to rouse the family from their sleep, getting into his car, backing out the driveway while hoping that no one could hear his tires crunching in the snow, and eventually making his way to the overpass.

"Yes it is quite a shock to everyone," I said. "And for you, it may be difficult helping Huy and Lien through their teenage years all by yourself." I imagined myself in her situation, suddenly alone to raise my spirited brood without my husband.

"Oh, I will manage. Huy is the man now. He will be in Duc's place. And Lien, she will help with the woman's work around the house because now I need to go back to work. We are a family, even without Duc." The little family nodded.

The Phams seemed to be in no visible distress. But I knew better. My first day back to high school after my brother died, I had wished that nobody knew what had happened so I could just be. I didn't want to have to worry about kids saying things that might hurt me even though they might have thought they were being kind and saying the right things. I didn't want anyone to look at me and to talk about what happened. If I smiled and pretended that all I wanted to do was catch up with my work, they would think that I was fine. I was anything but fine.

I wondered if Huy and Lien had felt any relief that Mr. Pham was out of their lives, burying his dark ruminations and obsessions with him. Maybe his demeanor had set a pall over the household and they had kept their own emotions hidden from him and each other, for fear they'd drive him further into despair.

I worried often about sweet Lien and stoic Huy and watched over them in the cafeteria, seeking any warning signs that they were struggling. But what I always saw was Lien laughing and whispering with her sixth-grade friends and Huy and his friends joking around and enjoying school. The guidance counselors called them in for occasional chats and said the kids were doing fine. Their teachers also reported that the kids were excelling academically.

After a couple of weeks had passed since the funeral, I called Mrs. Pham to see how everyone was doing and to offer any help they might need.

"We're doing quite well, thank you," she said. "The children are looking forward to the summer, when they can go to camp in Minnesota, and visit their grandparents who also live there," she said. "They've made a lot of friends there."

I told Mrs. Pham that I was glad things were going well for her and the children.

Yes, some people can do quite well, thank you. If that is their truth, they are lucky indeed.

"WE'LL STAY WITH YOU, MISS"

Analouisa and Louisiana helped me to continue teaching. I say this quite seriously. If it hadn't been for the inspiration they provided, I would have quit the profession.

I had been in the city for four years and I felt myself becoming increasingly frustrated. I didn't know who or what I was most angry about, but I knew that something had to change for me soon. The morale was very bad in the school—the kids were out of control, and we didn't have enough supplies.

What is the message that you get, whether you are child or staff, when you spend seven hours a day in a building that has a cafeteria fashioned out of a custodian's former supply closet that smells of curdling milk? When you have to provide your own toilet paper? When the "playground" is a parking lot?

It was no wonder that the kids and the staff were blue, unmotivated and anxious.

I was in a slump and I counted the days until the end of the school year. I ate unhealthy "comfort" food like chips and cake. My pants grew tighter and my mood got darker. It was only November and I wondered how I would make it to June.

One day, I was called into the principal's office. "We've got two new eight-graders, identical twin girls, fifteen-years-old, from New Orleans," said Joan, the principal. "The mother is still in New Orleans with her boyfriend. The dad is supposedly in the Dominican Republic but who knows."

"So who do they live with?" I asked.

"Their nineteen-year-old sister who's a high school senior, and their eighty-eight-year-old grandmother who's dying of cancer."

"So, I'm here because the twins need to be with me?"

"They're really, really cute," said Joan. "We have school records but there's little information. Typical south. Name, address, date of birth, but no progress reports, no attendance, no testing, no nothing. I'm guessing that they have special needs because of the conversation I had with them this morning. Looks like they're pretty limited, although the taller one, Louisiana, seems like she is a *little* more on the ball."

Even though these kids didn't have the proper documentation to be in my special education classes, Joan didn't seem bothered by it. Then again, it wasn't up to me to make sure that we were on the right side of the law. If I did do what I supposed to do according to the rules, by the time these kids were determined to be eligible for services, the school year would be over. Whenever I did something that I knew was not proper or legal, but needed to be done, I'd tell myself that I would be long-dead and buried before anyone figured out that I belonged in a jail for special educators. Better to be on the right side of the kid. My motto was that I'd rather ask for forgiveness than permission.

⇒⊦⊣⇐

The twins appeared at my classroom door after the first bell the next day.

Joan wasn't kidding when she said they were really cute. These two were stunning, like Naomi Campbell stunning. Their pert tiny noses and full lips were perfectly proportioned as though they had been sculpted.

"They tell us to come here," said Louisi, the taller of the two and more outspoken. I could barely hear her.

"Come in, girls. Welcome aboard. I'm so glad to meet you."

I introduced the girls to their classmates, signed out books for them and got them set for the school year. They nodded, they smiled, but neither said a word that day—or during the next two weeks.

Despite having the materials that they needed, they did very little work. I did my best to coax them to join in the classes, but they just smiled and doodled in their notebooks.

I had few options. I tried getting the grandmother involved, but there was no phone at home. I sent letters home—written in Spanish and English—that requested a meeting, but I heard nothing. Rick, the parent liaison, didn't speak Spanish and neither did I.

I suggested that the girls stay after school to do some work with me. I expected them to shake their heads or look down at their desks to avoid me. Louisiana looked at Analouisa, as though asking for her permission. Ana nodded.

After all the other kids had gone home, the girls remained at their desks. I sat facing them, to better facilitate a conversation.

"Girls, can you help me understand what's going on here? I've been trying for weeks now to have you participate in my class. What am I doing wrong?"

"Ana and me don't know how to read," said Louisi. "They try to teach us in New Orleans, but we can't learn. We want to drop out but we too young. One more year. Then we drop out."

Louisi rubbed her eyes, and when Ana saw that she was tearing, she patted her back.

I didn't know what to say. Maybe they were too cognitively impaired to read? Without testing results, I couldn't tell much about their abilities or even what Louisi meant by saying she couldn't read.

"Are you girls willing to try to learn again? We can try after school, after everyone has gone home. Every day. Just the three of us, working, working, and we'll try again. I bet that with just you two alone in the class, we can make some progress."

"We can try," Louisi said. "Ana and I need to learn."

"If we all do our best, girls, and work hard, I'm sure we can get where we want to be. Just stay every day and we'll work on your reading. Make sure you tell your grandmother that you'll be late coming home from school."

"We'll stay with you Miss," Louisi said.

I had made similar deals many times before, but inevitably, after two or three weeks, attendance would fall off. Most kids stopped coming because they had to babysit, cook for the family or lost interest.

To my pleasant surprise, Ana and Louisi never missed a day. We shared granola bars and bananas, worked on reading exercises and completed homework assignments. After they were tested, I discovered that both girls were cognitively impaired.

One frigid February night, their tenement house burned down and the Red Cross placed the family in the gym at the local Bennington School. This didn't seem to depress them. Louisi said she liked living with other families because she and Ana could play basketball at night, someone came to cook dinners and she loved having so much food. After a few weeks, the local newspaper wrote a story about their unusual living arrangements—Ana and Louisi were seated in the front row of the group picture, smiling, their heads leaning against each other. Ana held a basketball.

I admired these girls and wondered what made them so resilient in the face of adversity. Their optimism, their drive and their support for each other were a sharp contrast to what I saw in the middle-class suburb where I lived. These twins loved our old school. They were made of something that I wanted all the kids to have. I wanted some of what they had too.

⚔️

Grandma died the week after the eighth grade graduation dance. I hoped she had seen them dressed in their purple silk dresses, their hair wound into delicate buns. They were so beautiful inside and out.

The day after their grandmother's death, the girls announced that they were returning to New Orleans because their sister was going into the Marines and their mom said they could come back. I loved those girls. They had given me so much at a low point in my life, and I knew that I would really miss them.

Louisi was reading easy books by the time the girls graduated from the eighth grade. Ana had improved her sight word vocabulary, but I doubted that she would ever read at a functional level.

Most people who knew of my relationship with the twins gave me credit for their improvement—academically and socially. The real truth was that they prevented me from becoming a middle-school dropout.

"BEFORE YOU LEAVE..."

Someone knocked on my door. One gentle knock, followed by another more forceful knock.

I was on the phone and unhappy about this interruption but I covered the mouthpiece and said, "Come in!"

Barry, a seventh grade Social Studies teacher, opened the door a crack, stuck his head in, and asked, " OK to bother you?" He raised his eyebrows in askance even though he knew I'd never say no. "I'm on my break and I want to talk to you before you leave."

I was retiring from my assistant principal duties the very next day. "Sure, come in, I can spare a few minutes." I hung up the phone.

Barry was one of the few male teachers who wore a tie every day, and his shirts were always clean and crisp. Although he had never been in the military, Barry presented like a soldier with his perfect posture, spit-shined shoes and an unwillingness to waste time. He was also a rugged, tobacco-chewing high school football coach in a nearby town.

"Please, sit down." We sat at the conference table.

"Good to see you," I said. I felt my heart pounding. Barry and I had a history.

Barry's many strengths showed up my weaknesses. No detail had ever escaped his notice—his lesson plans were organized and comprehensive. His classroom was meticulously clean—books were lined up by height in his bookcase, desk chairs were pushed in after every class and there were no shavings under his pencil sharpener. He often shook his head when I allowed other teachers or faculty members to ramble on during meetings or if I allowed kids to leave classrooms randomly rather than in single file. Human beings were not perfect I reasoned, but he would argue that we could at least *try* to get them there.

"I'm here to tell you thank you, and I wanted to make sure that I told you in person before you left," he began. He smiled and cleared his throat. "I know that I'm probably the last person you expected to see from your fan club today."

I smiled.

"But I'm serious," he said. "I want to thank you for all that you taught me these last few years. I learned a lot from you. 'Pick your battles,' 'Don't sweat the small stuff,' 'Get the facts before you react,' 'Love the kids and they'll love you.'"

He extended his legs under the table and placed his hands on his thighs.

I knew that he had dreaded initiating this conversation, but now that he had, he was ready to relax.

"Well, thank you, Barry," I began. "I know it wasn't easy for you to work with me. Not a marriage made in heaven that's for sure. My less than stellar way of taking shortcuts and my sloppy organization skills drove you crazy I imagine. I certainly wouldn't describe myself as a role model in that department. Thank you. Your words mean a lot to me."

"Well, I gotta go," he said. "I'll miss you and I wish you all the best." He stood and pushed in his chair.

"Sure," I said. Barry opened the door to head back to class. "And Barry, thanks for coming by. I really appreciate your kind words. Truly."

During those last few days at work, many people stopped by my office to reminisce about the laughs we had shared or to rehash school stories. But it was the conversation with Barry that gave me the most satisfaction. I was thankful that despite our struggles, in the end, I had made a friend.

It was our last conversation. Barry died of a heart attack while camping in New Hampshire just a year after he had surprised me in my office, making my departure so sweet. He was 41 years old.

Made in the USA
Middletown, DE
29 July 2016